# children of the dawnland

also by w. michael gear and
kathleen o'neal gear

*Children of the Dawnland: Part One*

# children of the
# dawnland

Part Two

**W. Michael Gear**

**Kathleen O'Neal Gear**

**Children of the Dawnland: Part Two**
Paperback Edition
Copyright © 2024 (As Revised) W. Michael Gear
and Kathleen O'Neal Gear

Wise Wolf Books
An imprint of Wolfpack Publishing
701 S. Howard Ave. 106-324, Tampa, Florida 33609

wisewolfbooks.com



Maps and illustrations by Ellisa Mitchell.

eBook ISBN 978-1-957548-48-7
Paperback ISBN 978-1-957548-99-9

*To Tedi, Jessie, Ben, Shannon, and Jake*
*Our faithful friends and the purest hearts we've ever known.*

# children of the dawnland

Cobia's Cave
Hoarfrost Canyon
Oakbeam Village
Sunhawk Village
Starhorse Village
Clearwater Village
Screech Owl's Cave
Buffalobeard Village
N
Elisa Mitchell 2008

Ice Giants
ICE
ICE
ICE
ICE
ICE GIANT LAKE
Lands of the People of the Dawnland
Lands of the Thornback People
The People of the Dawnland's Villages
Oakbeam Village
Sunhawk Village
Starhorse Village
Clearwater Village
Buffalobeard Village
Screech Owl's Cave
Hoarfrost Canyon
and Cobia's Cave

# one

I 2,900 Years Ago, a time when mammoths and dire wolves trotted across the glacial wilderness that was America...

Halfmoon drew his buckskin cape more tightly about his shoulders and ducked beneath the flap into Chief Gill's lodge. Fifty hands across, it was the largest mammothhide lodge in Buffalobeard Village, and the most opulent. Hundreds of prayer feathers hung from the pole frame, twisting gently in the wind, and painted rawhide shields lined the walls. Each bore the colorful image of one of Gill's Spirit Helpers: Bear, Lion, and Condor. In the rear, a stack of buffalo hides the height of a man lay folded.

"Good evening," Halfmoon said, squinting. Though he saw better after Father Sun descended into the underworld at night, his vision was still blurry.

The three other elders already sat around the fire. The white-haired old women, Bandtail and Snapper, sat on either side of Gill. They both looked angry. Gill, on the other hand, looked tired. He had a golden elk hide over his shoulders.

"Good evening," Gill greeted them. "Please sit down and dip yourself a cup of tea."

Halfmoon sat on the buffalo hide near Bandtail. Though his vision was fading, he could still make out her bulbous nose and puckered mouth. She looked like she wanted to spit upon him for calling this late council session.

Gill gestured to Halfmoon. "Since you called us together to talk about your granddaughter's dreams, Halfmoon, please begin."

Halfmoon reached for the wooden cup and dipped it into the tea bag hanging on the tripod at the edge of the fire. The scent of tundra wildflowers rose. "Forgive me for being late. I've been speaking with our warriors most of today; then I met with my daughter, our Spirit dreamer, before coming here. She tells me that my granddaughter, Twig, is now studying with Screech Owl."

A sour expression came over Bandtail's face. "Yes, so?"

Halfmoon sipped his tea, stalling to allow them more time to think about what he'd just said. Their village had not sent a dreamer away to study for thirteen summers. It was a rare and important occasion, though the pinched expressions on Bandtail's and Snapper's faces told him they didn't seem to grasp that fact.

He sat up straighter, "I know this council decided that we should not pack up and move our village, but I must tell you that Twig has been having powerful Spirit dreams that should make this council reconsider."

"Bah!" Bandtail said. "She's too young to have Spirit dreams. She is not even a woman yet."

Halfmoon nodded. "I realize it is unusual for a child to have Spirit dreams so young. But do not forget that Cobia—"

Snapper interrupted, "Twig is not Cobia. Twig has always been a normal child. Cobia was terrifying from the instant you brought her here. If we'd been smart, we would have driven her away long before she had a chance to kill Minnow."

"Yes," Bandtail agreed. "Twig is just a girl. Power does not hover around her like it did Cobia."

Gill held up a hand, asking for silence. "Please, before we make any judgments, perhaps we should allow Halfmoon to tell us what his granddaughter has dreamed."

Bandtail and Snapper whispered to each other for a time; then Bandtail flicked a hand at Halfmoon. "Go on. Tell us."

Halfmoon set the wooden cup on a hearthstone before saying, "Twig has been having the same dream for some time. She sees a green flaming ball of light roll through the sky right over her head. Screech Owl told her that it might mean the Star People are going to make war on us."

Bandtail exhaled hard. "And what does young Twig suggest we do to stop this terrible event?"

"Twig thinks we should move west. As soon as possible."

Snapper leaned forward and shook a crooked finger at Halfmoon. "You've been trying to get us to move for over half a moon. The last time you told us we had to move south because the Thornback raiders were going to attack us. But that hasn't happened."

"Yet," Halfmoon said. "It hasn't happened *yet*, Snapper. I still believe they're coming. And if Twig's dreams are true, that is another reason we should —"

"They aren't true," Bandtail insisted. She folded her arms across her chest. "If Twig really is having Spirit dreams, then why hasn't our own village Spirit dreamer brought us this information? Hmm? She's your daughter! We had a village council meeting with her this very afternoon, and she said nothing about Twig having Spirit dreams. As far as I'm concerned, this discussion is over. You will never convince me that little Twig is a Spirit dreamer."

"I agree," Snapper said. "I think you are just trying another tactic to force us to move when we don't want to."

Halfmoon sighed. He had expected this. Bandtail and Snapper generally agreed, and once they'd made up their minds, there was little anyone could do to change them. "When my granddaughter returns from Screech Owl's, may I at least bring her to speak to the council? Perhaps if you hear about her dreams from her own lips, you will be more inclined to heed her words."

Gill looked around the circle, waiting to see if anyone else wished to speak, before he said, "My own opinion is that we should question the girl, as we do all potential Spirit dreamers. Do you agree?"

Bandtail grudgingly answered, "I will be happy to question her."

"So will I," Snapper said and grunted as she rose to her feet. "Though I think it is a waste of time."

"Then we are agreed." Gill looked around. "When Twig returns, we will question her and then decide whether or not we should reconsider our vote not to move the village."

Snapper made a disgusted sound and ducked under the lodge flap and out into the darkness.

Bandtail propped her walking stick and stood up. She glared at Halfmoon, and then she, too, left.

When they were alone, Halfmoon looked at Chief Gill. "Well, that was unpleasant. I had hoped they would listen carefully, even if they did not believe Twig was a Spirit dreamer."

Gill gave him a tired smile. "They are ten summers older than you or I. They have seen many would-be Spirit dreamers, and most have turned out to be simply children with imaginations. And..." Gill lifted both hands. "You've been pushing very hard to get us to move the village. They both naturally suspect you made up the story about Twig's dreams."

Halfmoon rose to his feet. "The fact that my own daughter, our village Spirit dreamer, has never mentioned Twig's dreams did not help my cause, either."

"No." Gill shook his head. "It didn't."

Halfmoon bowed politely to Gill, then ducked beneath the lodge flap into the night. The cold air smelled of damp earth and wet leather. All fourteen lodges had a golden glow from the fires burning inside, and he heard people talking and laughing.

As he made his way across the plaza, he knew he would not win this battle in the council unless either they were attacked by raiders, or Twig's dream came true.

And by then, it would be too late.

# two

For as far as I can see, darkness floods outward, rippling to the ends of the sky. My skin gleams blue-white in the eerie light. Runs In Light stops suddenly and points. "Do you see that, Twig?"

At the end of the blue web, a forbidding wall of ice rises.

Runs In Light trots forward.

"Wait! Where are you going? Don't go out there!"

"Let me show you. Hurry. Come this way." He races up to the top of the cliff and stands looking down into the massive crack.

"Stay back!" I shout. "It's too dangerous!"

"Not if you follow me," he says and leaps down.

I'm sobbing when I reach the place where he has vanished. But deep in the bottom, I see him. He is standing on a trail that runs between the steep ice walls.

"Come on, Twig. Follow me!"

I'm terrified, but I leap...

*And I land as softly as a feather. High above me, a clear patch of night sky shines.*

*"It's this way," he says.*

*As we run, the sky vanishes, and we enter a black tunnel.*

*"Through here." Runs In Light drops to his knees and scrambles forward. "This is the way, Twig."*

*I crawl through behind him. Darkness weighs down on me, heavy, taking my breath away while it pounds on my eardrums and presses on my eyelids.*

*But far ahead, I see a tiny spot of light. It grows larger as we near it.*

*I step out of the tunnel into the sunlight and inhale a deep breath of the chill, bright air. This world smells strange, as though moss and chokecherry had been steeping together for a thousand summers.*

*"Come, Twig. It's just a little farther."*

*Runs In Light clambers through the maze of boulders where Father Sun shines on his black braids. "Up here, Twig. Let me show you what happens when a dreamer fails."*

*I jump to the next boulder, following him. When I reach the top, I see herds of curious, hump-backed animals with long necks. Their ears and tails switch away flies while they inquisitively study us. Ice-capped mountains thrust up like teeth behind them.*

*"What are they?" I ask.*

*"Those are camels. They've only been gone for a short time." He lifts his arm and points to the south. "Do you see the people?"*

*I look, and there, I see people hunting. They have their prey trapped against a towering cliff. It might be a buffalo calf, but if so, the distance between the tips of its horns is three times as wide as the buffalo in my world, and it is much taller. The animal stamps its hooves and charges, trying to kill its attackers. People dodge and run, using their atlatls to launch long spears into its sides. The animal lets out a roar that sounds like a dying saber-toothed cat. Then, again, it makes a feeble run to scatter the humans. But they just circle and keep throwing their spears.*

*"Where are we?" I whisper.*

*Runs In Light crouches down. "This is the land of Giant Bison and Cheetah. That big buffalo down there is an orphaned bison calf. It's the last giant bison alive. Humans killed it's mother less than a moon ago. Now they're killing it."*

*"It's the last of its kind? Why don't you stop them?"*

*"We tried to. But when the One Life has been turned upside down, only a living dreamer can make it right again. Power finds the best dreamer it can—but sometimes the dreamer fails."*

*I kneel beside him, watching as the giant bison calf wails and drops to its knees. Even from this distance, I see the blood that froths at the animal's mouth. The calf shoves itself up on trembling legs but stumbles and falls on its side in the snow field. All of the people shout happily and hug each other as the bison calf's huge head sinks into the drift, and the snow runs red with its blood.*

*"How could they do that?" Tears make my voice tight. "Didn't they know it was the last giant bison alive?"*

*"No. But even if they had known, it wouldn't have made any difference. They are hungry. They need its meat." Runs In Light exhales hard. "That's what happens when the One Life is knocked out of balance. Earthmaker created*

*the universe to have equal portions of light and dark, pain and happiness, birth and death, heat and cold. But sometimes the world gets knocked out of balance...and the One Life falters."*

*Tears blur my eyes as I watch the hunters begin the hard work of butchering the beautiful bison calf. With sharp stone tools, they pull back the hide and carve off the rich red meat.*

*"You see that man on the far right? The one with Owl's face painted on his shirt?"*

*I wipe my eyes and nod. The man stands with his shoulders slumped forward, a hand braced on the head of a thin little girl who bounces joyfully up and down as she watches the piles of meat growing.*

*"His name is Tusk Boy. Power placed all of its strength and hope in him. He had Owl as a Spirit Helper from the day of his birth. But in the end, when Power called him to the river that runs before the Land of the Dead so he could learn how to set the One Life straight again, he couldn't do it. He was afraid to cross."*

*My mouth has gone dry. "Afraid he would drown?"*

*"Yes. He knew his starving wife and children needed him, and they meant more to Tusk Boy than Bison Calf did. Only a few dreamers are willing to sacrifice themselves, and their families, so that yellow butterflies may continue to flutter over the wildflowers in springtime. It is those few that Power seeks out. But not even Power can know for certain who will succeed and who will fail." Runs In Light gives me a sad smile. "No one really wants to be a dreamer, Twig. Not even you."*

*The grassy plains before me change, glittering like a swarm of gnat wings before fading into a new vision...*

# three

The long, deeply blue twilight of the Moon-When-Thunderbird-Walks settled over the land, bringing with it Wind Woman's fury. The gale had come up early that afternoon, roaring, blasting everything in its path, blowing the snow into deep drifts along the trails.

Greyhawk stood outside Screech Owl's cave, gripping his atlatl while he surveyed the drifts, and beyond them, the smoke that billowed across the western sky in a great purple smear. If he had his directions right, that was about the location of Clearwater Village. It was burning.

Yipper kept sniffing the air, whimpering, and gazing up at Greyhawk as though to say, *"Why are we still here? We have to go home."*

Greyhawk stroked Yipper's black head, but in the back of his mind, he was going over and over every lesson he had learned in warriors' school. How to hold his atlatl, how to make a good sharp spear point, how to cast, how to track an enemy across bare stone...how to survive when you were being chased by killers.

Screech Owl ducked out of the cave and followed Greyhawk's gaze. "Come back inside, Greyhawk. It's too cold to stand out here. Besides, there's nothing you can do."

Greyhawk turned to face him. The old man wasn't nearly as scary today. Instead, he looked frail and worried. Greyhawk pointed to the smoke with his atlatl. "Can you see that smoke?"

Screech Owl nodded. "Yes. I see very well far away."

"Do you think that's Clearwater Village?"

"Probably."

Greyhawk's stomach muscles knotted. "The Thorn-back raiders must have attacked just before the storm."

Wind Woman whipped long gray hair over Screech Owl's eyes. He squinted through it. "Yes, I pity the poor people who escaped the raid. The snow is so deep. They won't get far."

Greyhawk gripped his atlatl more tightly. He longed to be home near his father. The people in Buffalobeard Village must have seen the smoke early this morning. They would be packing up everything they owned, getting ready to abandon Buffalobeard Village as soon as the trails melted out.

Screech Owl asked, "Did you ever find out what happened to Puffer? At the Buffalo Way ceremony, all I heard was that she was dead."

Greyhawk looked westward to where the Ice

Giants gleamed in the dawn light. Cobia's cave was there somewhere...but Puffer had never even gotten close. "Puffer and her war-party were ambushed near the ruins of Starhorse Village. The warrior who escaped, Searobin, said that he never saw men, just black shapes floating through the trees."

"For black shapes, they cast their spears with deadly accuracy."

"Yes, and I—I have to get home, Screech Owl. Someone has to stop the Thornback raiders. Our village is going to need every warrior, even boys just learning to be warriors."

"Well, you can't go anywhere today. Perhaps tomorrow I'll take you and Twig home."

"You mean if Twig wakes up."

"Yes," Screech Owl softly answered.

Greyhawk leaned his shoulder against the ice-crusted boulder. All night long, Twig had moaned and thrashed, then she'd gone absolutely still. She hadn't moved at all today. She just lay lifelessly on the litter. Early that morning, Greyhawk had panicked and demanded that Screech Owl do something, so the old man had checked for a heartbeat, then had placed a mica mirror beneath her nose. Nothing.

Terrified, Greyhawk asked, "Is Twig dead? Did you kill her? You killed my best friend!"

Screech Owl ran a hand through his matted gray hair. "Greyhawk, I just wanted her to see the tunnel. I never thought she'd be able to—"

"To dream her way to the skyworld? She's a great dreamer! Didn't you know that?"

His words were torn away by Wind Woman and blown into the white distances.

Screech Owl tiredly folded his arms across his bony chest. The old man hadn't gotten much sleep last night. Every time Greyhawk had awakened, he'd seen Screech Owl sitting in his protective circle, staring at Twig. Throughout the long night, his face had grown more and more frightened.

"I thought she might just be able to peer over the edge into the darkness," Screech Owl explained. "It takes even the greatest dreamers many summers to gain the skill and courage to actually plunge into the spiraling black throat that carries them up to the skyworld."

"But she did it, didn't she?"

"Maybe."

The old man had been half-crazy all day, rushing around the cave, turning first one way, then back the other way, as though he were lost in a maze.

"Maybe Twig just decided to stay longer, to talk with her dead grandmother, or maybe her father?" Greyhawk suggested.

Screech Owl hesitated for a long time before he said, "It's possible. Many dreamers stay in the skyworld for days, talking to Spirits, visiting with old friends. But Twig is so young..." Guilt twisted his face.

A kestrel soared through the sky high above, shrieking before swooping low over the boulders. Screech Owl shielded his eyes to watch its flight. He didn't seem to recognize the bird. For good measure, Yipper growled at it.

"Can't you try to wake her?" Greyhawk asked.

"If she hasn't awakened by tomorrow morning, I'll try brewing a Spirit tea to bring her home. But danger lurks in even the slightest interference. If Twig is struggling against some Spirit creature and I so much as call her name, the distraction could cause her doom. But if she had an accident, if her litter overturned and she's drowning...well, she would be running through a country that has no landmarks...a country haunted by horrors you cannot even imagine. In that case, my voice might help lead her home."

"Why can't you just go after her and bring her back?"

Screech Owl's hands dropped limply to his sides. "The skyworld is vast. Every dreamer enters at a different place. It spreads out infinitely in all directions. Finding her would take a miracle."

Greyhawk's gaze returned to the streaks of gray that drifted across the heavens. What was happening out there? Elder Halfmoon must already be in war council, planning what to do. The snow would slow the raiders down, but...

"The Thornback raiders will be coming for us next, Screech Owl. We have to stop them."

# four

I ce and snow gust by, making it almost impossible for me to see anything...Then, a young man appears, standing on the crest of an ice ridge. He wears a white bear hide over his shoulders, and long black hair whips around his face.

Standing alone on the ice, the young man cries, "I'm not the one! I'm no dreamer."

"Who is he?" I ask Runs In Light. "Wolf Dreamer. He succeeded. He—"

"Wolf Dreamer! Is that who he is? He's one of the Blessed Hero Twins."

"Yes, he dreamed humans into the land where you live, even though all he wanted was to be a hunter and to raise a family with the woman he loved."

"Power wouldn't let him?"

"He wouldn't let himself. The survival of Life was more important to him than his own wants. Without his dream, humans would never have found the way to your world."

I clench my fists. "So Wolf Dreamer was brave enough?"

"Yes, but not until the very end."

Runs In Light turns to look at me. His young face has taken on a bittersweet expression that melts my heart. Snow blasts by us, whistling, freezing on our eyelashes.

"No one wants to be a dreamer, Twig. But someone must be."

I force a swallow down my throat. "I'm afraid, but... I'll try. Can you help me? I've only seen twelve summers."

"So had I," he says softly. "I had seen twelve summers when Power called."

"You were a dreamer?"

"Yes. A very long time ago."

Runs In Light rises to his feet, and the air wavers around him, blurring his body into bizarre, ominous shapes. "It was even harder for me than it is for you, Twig. I was more afraid than you can imagine."

"How did you get over it?"

"I united the worlds of Animal and Human in myself and became my Spirit Helper."

"Became?"

"Some dreamers are strengthened when they are consumed by fire. Other dreamers need water. Some, like us, have to drown in blood before they can unite worlds inside themselves. Don't fear it, Twig. That crushing beak will give you wings."

"What do you mean? I don't understand."

I stumble backward when Runs In Light's legs begin to writhe in a hideous dance. As I watch, black fur sprouts from his skin, and he turns into a wolf—a big, black wolf. With wistful, human eyes, he peers up at me. "You and

*Greyhawk must go to Cobia's cave. Eagle-Man waits for you there."*

*The wolf lopes away at full speed, charging through the icy wilderness as though being chased by an invisible monster.*

*"Runs In Light, wait! How do I get home? I can't get home!"*

*In a voice that grows fainter by the instant, he calls, "Go and ask Wolf Dreamer."*

*I turn to look at the man standing on the crest of the ridge. He's smiling at me, but he looks sad.*

*As I climb toward him, he calls, "Hurry, Twig. The Thornback raiders are approaching your village. Very soon, they will find your family. You must hurry. Hurry."*

# five

Greyhawk and Screech Owl continued to stare out across the white wasteland of snow toward the burning village in the distance. The smoke had started to coil upward like a black tornado.

Screech Owl said, "You are right, Greyhawk. We must stop them, but—" He stopped and cocked an ear.

A soft mewing rose, so faint it barely carried over the wind.

Then Greyhawk clearly heard a cough and a wheezed, "Screech Owl?"

*"Twig?"*

Screech Owl dashed beneath the leather curtain, and Greyhawk ducked into the cave behind him.

Twig was lying on her side, her body dripping wet. Strange bits of moss clung to her sleeves. She coughed again, desperately, and tried to raise herself on her elbows but weakly fell back against the fox hides.

Greyhawk cried, "Twig! Are you all right?"

Screech Owl ran for her, scooped her up in his arms, and frantically kissed her soaked face. "Thank Earthmaker, I was so afraid."

Yipper trotted over to sniff Twig's head, then licked her arm affectionately. She didn't seem to feel it. She kept coughing.

Greyhawk didn't know what to do. He just stood rigidly, clutching his atlatl, waiting to hear her speak. She looked different somehow, her eyes brighter, and not quite human.

Twig fell into a violent coughing fit. A trickle of water ran from her mouth. She fought to catch her breath and started choking. Screech Owl laid her facedown on the floor and firmly pressed against her back. More water gushed from her lungs, forming a small, crystalline pool on the hides. He pressed again and again, until she seemed to be breathing easily; then, he stretched out on the floor beside her to study her face. She smiled weakly. Screech Owl lifted a hand and stroked her sopping hair. "Are you feeling better?"

"Yes," she whispered.

Greyhawk knelt beside her. His throat had closed up, making it hard to breathe. "I thought you were dead," he said. "I missed you badly."

Her pretty face, with its full lips and straight nose, had gone as white as the snow. But her eyes gazed at him steadily. "I fell into the river."

"The river that runs in front of the Land of the Dead? How did you get out?"

"I was...was drowning. I saw something in the waves. It came and slithered inside me."

"Snake?" Greyhawk hissed in surprise.

She nodded. "Water Snake. I—I got Water Snake's soul. Then... I could swim to shore."

Screech Owl said, "That's good, Twig. You wanted Water Snake's soul. How did—"

"Runs In Light came...came to..." She started coughing again.

"Wait, Twig," Screech Owl said gently, seeing how hard it was for her to talk. "You need to rest and eat. We'll talk about these things when you're stronger."

Twig nodded, and her hand crept spiderlike across the floor until she could twine her fingers in Screech Owl's buckskin shirt. "I tried very hard...to come back to you. I love you, Screech Owl. You, too...Greyhawk."

Screech Owl stroked her hair. "We love you, too, Twig. You sleep now. When you wake up, we'll eat and talk."

# six

Wind.

And more wind, howling through the cold moonlight.

Twig watched Screech Owl crouch before the rabbit that was skewered on a long stick and propped near the flames. He turned the stick so the rabbit would cook on the other side and then glanced at Twig. She sat across the fire pit from him. Screech Owl had given her one of his old shirts to wear. It was much too big for her, but it was dry and warm. It was painted green with red spirals and black dancing bears. Screech Owl had explained that it had come from his ritual attire and had been specially blessed by Kestrel Above.

"Twig?" Greyhawk said. "Can you talk now?"

She nodded, but didn't say anything. Her gaze was fixed on the snowflakes that blew past the cave entrance. They were whispering to each other, but she couldn't understand their words.

Screech Owl dipped a horn-spoon into the pot of tea, stirring it for the twentieth time.

Greyhawk walked over and knelt beside Screech Owl to whisper, "Why isn't she talking?"

Screech Owl said, "That happens to dreamers when they get new souls. They become disoriented for a time, seeing an old world through strange new eyes. I've known dreamers who went mad from fear. And others who left their homes and families and just ran away into the forest, never to be seen again."

"Did that happen to you?"

"Me? No, of course not. I was delighted by the bizarre thoughts that came to me. After I got Pack Rat's soul, I had the urge to poke my nose into dark crevices looking for shiny objects. I didn't realize how dangerous it was. One night, I poked my head into a hole in the ground where Weasel lived, and Weasel sank his teeth into my nose. See this scar?" Screech Owl pointed to the white scar on his nose.

Greyhawk scowled.

Twig smiled and studied Screech Owl as he duck-walked to the rear of the cave to sift through the basket of dried blossoms. The delicate, flowery scent swirled up when he grasped a handful. He brought them back and stirred the blossoms into the boiling blend of roots.

"I saw Wolf Dreamer," Twig said.

"You *saw* the Blessed Hero Twin?" Greyhawk asked in awe.

"Yes, in the Land of the Long Dark. Have you ever seen him, Screech Owl?"

"No." Screech Owl cocked his head. "But each dreamer meets different Spirit Helpers in the skyworld."

Twig clasped her hands in her lap. "After Runs In Light left me, I didn't know how to get home, so I walked down to Wolf Dreamer. We talked. He told me things..."

She understood why a new dreamer might go mad. The things she'd seen were terrifying and magical. The colors were almost too dazzling to look at, and the faces of the Spirits shone as though coated with liquid moonlight.

Greyhawk said, "What did he tell you, Twig?"

She blinked at the swaying door-curtain. She didn't know if she should answer. Besides, a silence lived in her heart now—a deep, bright silence that was perfectly calm. She longed to swim in it forever.

Screech Owl filled three wooden cups with tea, then slid the rabbit into a bowl and tore off the legs. He handed a teacup and a bowl with a leg to Greyhawk, then carried Twig's teacup and bowl over and set them by her knees. She barely saw him.

Screech Owl picked up his own dinner and gently said, "First, tell us about the journey, Twig. Did Eagle-Man come up through the tunnel in the spruce branch?"

"Yes," she said softly. "He brought the Spirit buffalo. They put their heads through the nooses you made. Then...then we started up...flying into the dark storm."

Steam rose around Screech Owl's face as he

sipped his tea. "Eat while you talk, Twig. You must be starving."

She picked up her rabbit leg and chewed it thoughtfully while her gaze touched each sacred symbol painted on the walls. The spirals and purple starbursts glittered in the firelight.

"The buffalo had a hard time pulling the litter through the river, Screech Owl."

"They always do. It's so deep and wide."

"And fast. It rushed so fast."

"So you fell in and had to turn back?"

She finished chewing and swallowed. At the memory, fear, like a living thing, coiled in her belly. "Yes."

Screech Owl sat forward and gently touched her shoulder. "That's all right, Twig. You did well."

"But I didn't make it across to the Land of the Dead. I'm sorry."

In a hushed voice, Screech Owl said, "Don't be. Very few Spirit dreamers ever reach the Land of the Dead. Especially on their first try."

Greyhawk looked at Screech Owl. "How long did it take you to make it across the river?"

The old man cocked his head. "I finally made it on my fifteenth try. I'd seen twenty-two summers."

Twig continued, "But I could see things on the other side: old fire pits, stumps with ax marks. And the trees, the trees, Screech Owl! They were so tall their tops disappeared into the clouds. That's when Runs In Light led me to the Long Dark. And...and I met Wolf Dreamer."

Twig gobbled a chunk of meat, barely chewing

it; then she lowered her eyes, and tears glistened on her lashes. "The Thornback raiders are coming, Screech Owl. Very soon."

"I knew it!" Greyhawk shouted. "We have to go home!"

Screech Owl's eyes narrowed, as though in pain. "Did Wolf Dreamer tell you how to stop them?"

Twig didn't answer. She watched Screech Owl with the bright, unblinking eyes of Water Snake.

It must have scared Greyhawk. He walked across the cave to the entrance and pulled the curtain aside to stare out at the dark night, as though afraid he'd find Thornback raiders camped right outside. The faint scents of mud and soaked rocks blew in on Wind Woman's breath.

"Our families are in danger," Greyhawk said. "We have to get home. I'm leaving tomorrow at dawn. I don't care how deep the snow is."

Twig blinked. Only a few days ago, he'd been afraid of everything—birds, bullies, and fights. But now, he sounded like a warrior.

Screech Owl responded, "I'll take you. I don't want you going alone. If the raiders are out there, I—"

"Screech Owl?" Twig set her cup down and wrapped her arms around her knees. Her heart felt luminous. "Why didn't you ever tell me you were my father?"

Greyhawk's gaze shot to Screech Owl. "You...*you* are Twig's father?"

Screech Owl's hand stopped midway in bringing his teacup to his mouth. He seemed to be fighting to swallow past the knot in his throat. Tea sloshed onto the floor when he set his cup down. "Twig...I... your mother...she—she left me. She told me she never wanted to see me again after the dreams I had made her see. She hated me. She thought it would be better if people believed that Shouts-At-Night was your father. She said it would make things easier for you. I wanted to tell you so many times."

"But you're my father. Our people trace descent through the men. You could have made a claim on me."

"Yes," he said gently, "but I loved your mother. I didn't want to hurt her. And I—I thought you would be better off with her than me. I tried to see you every time I went to Buffalobeard Village. I've always loved you."

Twig gave Screech Owl an affectionate smile, and emotion seemed to swell at the back of his throat. He couldn't speak. He just tilted his head awkwardly, and Twig jumped up and hugged him.

"I'm glad you're my father, Screech Owl. There's nobody else I'd want for a father."

Greyhawk leaned against the cave wall as though he was a little faint. "I feel like someone just kicked me in the belly. Twig, are you sure? Who told you Screech Owl was your father?"

As the flames died down in the fire pit, smoke curled upward in billowing clouds, where it crept along the ceiling until it was sucked out through the crack.

Twig sat down again. "When I was drowning, I called out for my father, and I saw Screech Owl's face. Then, Wolf Dreamer told me that's where I get my ability to dream—from Screech Owl." She smiled at him. "I don't know why I didn't think of it myself."

Screech Owl said, "What else did he tell you, my daughter?"

Twig's soul seemed to be floating, moving with the dance of the firelight. She took a deep breath. "Screech Owl, Greyhawk, you have to promise not to tell anyone."

"I promise," Greyhawk said.

"As do I. What did he say?"

Twig exhaled hard. "We have to go find Cobia. Greyhawk and me. We have to do it together."

Greyhawk's knees went weak. "Me? Why do I have to go? I'm no dreamer!"

Twig whispered, "No, you're a warrior."

Screech Owl seemed to stop breathing. He stared hard at Greyhawk. "Yes, and you're about to be tested."

"Tested? What does that mean?" Greyhawk said.

"It means that Twig's Spirit Helper has called you. And having a Spirit Helper call you is a little like meeting Grandfather Grizzly unexpectedly in the dark forest. You never know whether he'll lead you out of the darkness to the trail home—or force you to run for your life."

Greyhawk started shaking his head and backing away, and Twig said, "Greyhawk, our families are in trouble. The Thornback raiders are headed for our village. My Spirit Helpers told me the only way we can really save our people is by finding Cobia."

He nervously licked his lips. "I'm ready to fight raiders, Twig, but Cobia..."

"Fighting the raiders won't be enough," Twig said softly. "There's something much worse coming. That's what we have to stop."

"The ball of light in your dream?"

"I think so. I—I don't understand what all of it means, Greyhawk. I just know we have to find Cobia."

Greyhawk gripped his atlatl and squared his shoulders. Yipper leaped to his feet as though he knew that meant they would be going soon. Greyhawk took a deep breath, and when he let it out, he said, "All right, Twig. If it means we can save our people, I'll go."

Twig nodded and started to say something, but she heard a whisper. Her gaze went to the colorful symbols painted on the walls, and she frowned, listening to them talking to each other. They had sweet, high voices. After ten heartbeats, she said, "We'll leave at dawn."

# seven

"**G**ET UP!"

The hoarse voice brought Hook straight out of a deep sleep. Dry Cloud screamed as Hook threw off his hides, grabbed his war club, and jumped to his feet, ready to club his enemy to death.

"I know where the Stone Wolf is."

Hook blinked. The dark silhouette of a man filled his entryway. Cold wind blew in, fluttering the scalps tied to the frame poles. The man was holding the lodge curtain open, and his body looked utterly black against the bright moonlight.

Breathlessly, Hook said, "My chief? Is that you?"

"The Stone Wolf is in Buffalobeard Village. Find it. And bring me the girl who has it. Leave now."

The curtain fell closed, and darkness filled the lodge.

"Blessed Spirits," Dry Cloud gasped. "What's he talking about?"

"Father?" his oldest son, Blue Dog, called. "Is everything all right?"

"Where are you going, Father?" Slate called, and then his entire family started talking at once, asking questions. Dry Cloud rose and walked across the lodge to check on Slate.

Hook's chest was heaving. He fought to force the blood surging in his veins to slow down.

"Quiet. I have to go assemble a war-party. I'll return as soon as I can."

# eight

Twig tugged up the hem of her green dress —actually, Screech Owl's ritual shirt with the dancing bears—to avoid the tangle of old roots that crept across the path. She had pinned her braid on top of her head with a wooden comb, but Wind Woman had torn loose straggles that blew before her eyes. In the pack on her back, she carried all of the sacred things that Screech Owl had used to teach her, a hollow tube to blow away evil Spirits, and her atlatl, plus the clothes she had brought with her. Screech Owl had made a special belt pouch for her to carry the spruce bough from First Woman's tree and told her *never* to lose it.

Five paces ahead of her, Screech Owl walked beside Greyhawk. Greyhawk carried his spear nocked in his atlatl, ready for a fight. He had been pensive all morning while they followed the winding trail that led to Buffalobeard Village. As the warmth of the day increased, more and more snow melted from the trail, leaving it muddy and slippery.

Greyhawk said, "Screech Owl, I've been wondering about finding Cobia's cave. I don't even know which trail to take. Do you?"

"You follow the lakeshore trail until you see an ice canyon, Hoarfrost Canyon; then you walk into the canyon. It gets more and more narrow as you go. At the end of the canyon, you'll see her cave."

"So, once we enter Hoarfrost Canyon, we can't miss it."

"That's right. Hoarfrost Canyon dead-ends at Cobia's cave. That's what makes it a perfect ambush place. The only way out is the way you came in."

"Then, if someone blocks the mouth of the canyon, we're trapped."

"Yes, though there are smaller caves that dot the ice cliffs..."

Twig barely heard them. She'd been thinking about her Spirit journey to the skyworld. Memories of her litter overturning in the river had been haunting her. In her nightmares, she still gulped mouthfuls of chilling water and felt her lungs go cold before she saw Water Snake slithering toward her.

"Screech Owl?" she asked. He and Greyhawk turned to look back at her.

"Yes, Twig?"

"What happens if I get Rock's soul before I have to go back into the skyworld?"

"What?"

"I asked, what happens if I have to cross the river in the skyworld with Rock's soul in my body?"

Greyhawk squinted at her. "Rock's soul?"

"Yes. You know, or something else that would sink. I'm worried that—"

"Oh...Oh, I understand. Well," Screech Owl gestured airily, "I suppose you'll have to roll along the river bottom until you find a firm enough place to roll ashore. You'll want to avoid all the mucky places of course, because if you get stuck, you won't have any hands or feet to push out with. Not having eyes will be the real problem, since you won't be able to see where you're going. But I suspect that if you feel your way, paying attention to the flow of the current, you'll make it." His bushy gray brows lifted abruptly. "That is, unless one of the grouse with fish fins dives down to gobble you up for its gizzard."

Greyhawk said, "I hope no worm souls try to get Twig before she has to talk to Eagle-Man again. Eagles love worms."

"That's not funny, Greyhawk," she said.

"And, then," Screech Owl tilted his head, "the other solution is just to cross the river in a different place. A place where it isn't as wide or deep. That will take some searching, of course. You might want to try a place up north, in the heart of the Ice Giants. Cobia once told me the river isn't nearly as wide there."

Twig frowned and walked up the trail. As she shifted the weight of her pack, the hollow tube for blowing away evil Spirits rattled. "Cobia won't kill us, will she?"

He tilted his head uncertainly. "No one can say what Cobia will or will not do. I just wish I knew how much time I have left to teach you. I don't want to push you, but, Twig—"

"We'd better do it, Screech Owl." She bit her lip, recalling the terror she'd felt when her litter had overturned in the sacred river. She could still see the faces of the buffalo as they dragged her litter away... and feel the icy water filling her lungs. Could she stand that again? "It might take me longer to learn than we expect."

Screech Owl trudged up a small rise that overlooked Ice Giant Lake. Far in the distance, Twig saw Buffalobeard Village nestled at the base of the rocky ridge. They had almost finished the rock wall. Only one gap remained on the south side of the village. The smoke from the campfires rose into the turquoise sky.

Twig thought she could see fishing boats out on the water and people moving along the lakeshore, but windblown snow blurred the distances. It might just be boulders. Still, her eyes lingered on those black dots, and her heart ached for her mother.

Greyhawk said, "Come on. Let's hurry. Even if we run all the way, we're not going to get home until after dark!"

Twig trotted down the hill behind Screech Owl and Greyhawk, calling, "When can you teach me more? Tonight?"

"If your mother will let me, yes. In fact, doing

this lesson in your own lodge might be best. You'll feel safer there than anywhere else."

Twig broke into a hard run, her legs pumping while the pack slapped her back. Ahead, the trail wound downward. "What will you teach me, Screech Owl?"

His sweat-damp gray hair flopped around his ears with each step. "I'm going to teach you how to cross the river and enter the Land of the Dead, Twig."

"After I cross the river, what do I need to do?"

Screech Owl caught up with her and put a hand on her shoulder to stop her. For a while, they just stood in the trail and looked at each other.

Then Screech Owl said, "After you cross the river, you have to step into the mouth of the Spirit that wants to chew you up."

# nine

Dusk was deepening into night when Twig made the last turn in the trail and ran headlong for home. As she crested a rise, she saw Buffalobeard Village. The circle of lodges still stood around the central fire pit, but big packs had been piled outside the lodges. From the looks of things, they would be leaving tomorrow.

Mother ducked out of their lodge, and Twig yelled, "Mother? Mother, I'm home!"

Mother turned and ran toward Twig. She had braided her hair and coiled it on top of her head, pinning it with a rabbit-bone pin. The style made her narrow face seem longer and her nose more hooked. Her shell-bead necklace glittered. "Twig? Oh, Twig! And Greyhawk! We were so worried about you!"

"I'm fine," Greyhawk said.

"Well, you'd better get home and tell your father. Right now. He's been terrified."

Greyhawk lifted a hand, called, "I'll see you in the morning, Twig," and raced across the village for his lodge.

Mother threw her arms around Twig and hugged her tightly. It felt so good to be close again. Mother kissed Twig's hair and face, and Twig's soul ached with happiness. "Oh, Mother, I missed you."

"And I missed you. Let me look at you. Are you all right?"

Twig's pack made her so awkward that she staggered sideways when Mother released her.

"Mother, guess what? I went into the skyworld! Screech Owl made a death litter for me, and Eagle-Man brought Spirit buffalo to pull it."

Mother smiled. "Yes, I made that same journey when I studied with Screech Owl. I think every dreamer in history has tried to make that trip. How far did you go? Did you get out of the cave?"

Excitedly, she said, "Oh, yes, I made it to the river, but my litter overturned, and I fell into the water—"

"You..." Mother blinked and lifted her gaze to Screech Owl, who had come to stand behind Twig. Twig saw Screech Owl nod, and Mother stroked Twig's hair in amazement. "I'm so proud of you, Twig. I tried many times to make it across the river. In fact, I've known only one dreamer in my life who has made it to the river and crossed it into the Land of the Dead." She looked at Screech Owl.

"Yes, well," Twig blurted happily, "Runs In Light told me that if I try very hard, I may be as great a dreamer as my father, Screech Owl—"

"*What?*" Mother's smile faded, then hardened into anger.

A dreadful silence fell. Twig's eyes went back and forth between them.

"I kept my promise, Riddle," Screech Owl said softly. "I didn't tell her. Her Spirit Helpers did."

Mother lowered her eyes disbelievingly before she said, "We'll discuss it later. I'm sure Twig is hungry. I have a fresh pot of grouse stew in our lodge."

Mother marched away, and Screech Owl patted Twig's head as he passed by her to catch up with Mother. "Riddle, please, let's talk now," he said; then his voice went too low for Twig to hear, but she could see Mother's shoulder muscles knot.

They marched staight back to Mother's lodge, whispering furiously.

The old people watched Twig as she followed along behind Mother and Screech Owl. She could see the curiosity in their weathered faces and knew they wanted to ask her what she'd learned. They were probably worried she didn't have a human soul —which, of course, she didn't.

Mother raised her voice to a shout. "I told you I didn't want her to know about you. We had a bargain! What am I going to do now?"

"Lower your voice, Riddle," Screech Owl pleaded.

Twig felt ill. She had been so afraid of telling Mother about having Water Snake's soul that she had forgotten she wasn't supposed to know about

Screech Owl being her father. What would happen because of her slip?

By the time she reached the lodge doorway, the barest sliver of Moon Maiden's face had peeked over the eastern horizon.

# ten

Twig sat on her bedding hides with her chin propped atop her knees. The Stone Wolf was whispering to the yellow spider painted on Mother's medicine bundle. She strained to understand the words. Strange that she had never heard them talking before. But Power was loose on the night. She could feel it nipping at her skin with tiny fangs.

She fiddled with the sleeves of Screech Owl's green ritual shirt, tugging at the fringes while she studied Screech Owl and Mother. They sat cross-legged near the fire.

If Twig had to listen to their silence much longer, she wouldn't be able to breathe. What had they said to each other on the way to the lodge? Something bad. Mother's face looked stormy as she filled bowls with grouse stew. Screech Owl wasn't looking at her. Instead, he was drawing magical signs on the hard-packed dirt floor.

Is that what the Stone Wolf and the spider were discussing? Their voices had dropped even lower.

Twig turned to watch the lodge flap sway in the wind. Every now and then, when Wind Woman shoved the flap open, she glimpsed Moon Maiden's face sitting above the rocky ridge. The tumbled boulders stood like dark sentinels against the silver undercoat of moonlight.

"Riddle," Screech Owl said very softly, and Twig took a deep breath. "You don't have to believe us, but—"

"I don't believe you," Mother responded in a low, shaky voice. Anger and hurt flashed in her eyes. "I think you've taught Twig enough. Maybe I won't let her go back to see you ever again!"

The deep wrinkles around Screech Owl's eyes tightened. "Dreamers are not made in a few days, Riddle. If Twig has to learn on her own, the pain will probably drive her away from dreaming. Power has chosen her. This is not something you or I have a say in. She will be a Spirit dreamer. The only choice we have is whether or not to help her. If we leave her to stumble around trying to find her own way—"

"Some people do better stumbling around than being guided by a crazy old fool."

Tears stung Twig's eyes. She just wanted Screech Owl to teach her for a little while longer—she didn't want to hurt Mother.

Mother tramped across the lodge, tugged the Stone Wolf from her medicine bundle, then walked back and knelt before Twig. The Wolf had a new leather thong on it, turning it into a necklace.

Mother's eyes looked blacker than black when she said, "See this, Twig? I made this so you could wear it when you got home." She draped the thong over Twig's head.

Twig shuddered when the Stone Wolf fell over her heart. Threads of power seeped from the Wolf and soaked into her chest. She barely heard Mother say, "The Wolf will help Twig, Screech Owl. She no longer needs you."

"But Riddle..."

A ragged scream shredded the night.

Screech Owl whirled around to look at the door-curtain.

Just when he started to rise, war cries rose out of nowhere. The high-pitched shrills slipped up and down like someone playing a bone comb with a chokecherry stick.

Someone cried, *"It's the Thornback raiders! Grab your weapons!"*

Screech Owl dove for the door, jerked the flap aside, and peered out at the night.

Twig could see them, and she knew immediately that she was too late! Too late to tell Grandfather or the elders what she'd learned. Too late to save them!

As the raiders ran through the village, casting their flaming spears into the lodges, they looked like black scraps of cloth flying in the wind. Lodges burst into flames, and people scrambled out to run.

The ghostly black raiders yipped and fell on the

old men, women, and children alike, chasing them down.

A flaming spear landed on the roof of Twig's lodge.

"Fire!" Mother screamed. Smoke rose in a gray haze and started to fill the lodge. "Screech Owl, our lodge is on fire!"

"Riddle, grab Twig! We'll have to break through the poles on the back of the lodge to get out."

"But they'll be watching!" Mother cried in terror. "You know they will. They're probably waiting for us to—"

"It's our only chance!"

Twig shouted, "Look!" and pointed at the roof.

Screech Owl lunged for Twig and knocked her back against the wall as a burning section of roof poles toppled into the lodge.

When Twig sat up, she saw Mother's arm twisted at an impossible angle in the midst of the flames. "Screech Owl. Save Mother! Help Mother!"

The fire roared, searing Screech Owl's face until he had to close his eyes. Roughly, he grabbed Twig's hand, dragged her to the back of the lodge, and jerked the frame poles apart. "Run and hide, Twig!" he shouted as he shoved her outside. "If I don't come to find you soon, remember what your Spirit Helpers have told you. Their words may save all of us!" He leaped back into the burning lodge.

Twig stood rigid, staring at her lodge. In terror, she cried, "Screech Owl! Mother! Where are you?"

No one answered.

Twig put her hands over her mouth to stifle her sobs and dashed out into the night.

Everywhere, dark, eerie warriors were chasing after running, screaming people.

Twig climbed up into the rocks, trying to find a good place to hide. Firelight reflected across the boulders, swirling like monstrous creatures with fiery wings.

Twig stumbled over a rock, regained her balance, and ran again until she could crawl into a thick brier of old bushes, where she fell to her knees. She watched in horror as enemy warriors shoved Screech Owl through the village plaza. He was carrying Mother in his arms. Her body, legs dangling, hung limply. She watched until they disappeared into the darkness. Was Mother dead?

A fist tightened around Twig's heart. *Mother? Mother, don't leave me!*

Twig gasped desperate breaths of the cold, smoky air while she tried to spot anyone else she knew. Warriors floated around the charred skeletons of lodges.

"Greyhawk, where are you? Eagle-Man, let him be all right. Oh, Grandfather. Grandfather, where are you?"

Twig crawled to the far end of the brush to see the village from a different angle, and she spied eight raiders creeping through the darkness. They seemed to be checking the base of the rocks for survivors. They flushed a mouse that darted away into the firelight crevices; then Old Man Blood Duck jumped out and tried to run on his maimed leg. One of the raiders pounced on him and clubbed him in the head. The old man crumpled to the ground like a rabbit-fur doll. Twig's heart thundered.

*They're going to find me. I have to run. But if I stand up, they'll see me. What...*

Suddenly, she knew. She flopped on her stomach and slithered through the brush, as silent as Water Snake, her movements hidden by the wavering dance of shadows.

# eleven

Greyhawk hid behind the low rock wall west of Buffalobeard Village, watching the lodges burn. All around him, ash fell like black snowflakes. Raiders stalked around, kicking dead bodies, spearing the wounded to make sure they would not rise again. Groans and hideous shrieks rang out.

Greyhawk was shaking so badly he could barely stand.

Yipper, who stood at his side, let out a low growl, and Greyhawk panicked. He grabbed Yipper's jaws hard and held them together, hissing, "No! Don't make a sound!"

Yipper stared up at him with wide eyes, but he seemed to understand. When Greyhawk let go, Yipper sat on his haunches and kept quiet.

Greyhawk moved along the boulders until he could see farther to the east. The raiders had captured several children. He saw Rattler, Buzzard,

Little Cougar, and Black Locust huddling together. Two men guarded them. The raiders must be planning on marching them home as slaves. Where were the other children? He saw two dead boys lying on the far side of the village, near the stone wall. Who were they? Which friends?

Ten paces away from the children, Screech Owl sat with seven adults. The old man had his shoulders hunched, staring down at the woman who lay unconscious across his lap. Twig's mother? Greyhawk couldn't see very well, but he thought that's who it was.

"Where's Father?" he whispered to himself. "Where's Elder Halfmoon, Searobin, and our other warriors? Where's Twig?"

He didn't see any of them, alive or dead.

Raiders encircled the villagers, holding their nocked atlatls up, ready to cast. Only one raider stood inside the circle with the villagers...and he was big. Tall, muscular, and dressed all in black, he looked like one of the giants from the Old Stories. All of the raiders had covered their faces with soot. The only thing Greyhawk could make out clearly was their eyes, shining in the firelight.

The big raider walked over and kicked Screech Owl hard in the ribs. "You, what's your name?"

"Screech Owl. What's yours?"

Had the old man's eyes and beaked nose grown bigger? They seemed enormously large in the thin frame of his face. His tan shirt was filthy, covered with dark streaks of charcoal.

"What do you know about a Spirit object called

the Stone Wolf? It's supposed to live in Buffalobeard Village. Have you ever heard of it?"

"Oh, yes," Screech Owl said, mopping his forehead with his torn sleeve. "It did live here, many summers ago. But it vanished."

"What do you mean it vanished?"

"Someone stole it. Quite a long time ago. Isn't that what happened, Riddle?"

The woman lying in his lap turned to glower at the big raider. Her mouth moved, but Greyhawk couldn't hear her answer. Her voice must be very weak. At least she was alive.

The big raider slapped his atlatl against his leg. "I don't believe you. Our chief told us there was a Stone Wolf here and that it possessed great power."

"Well, if it was here," Screech Owl remarked reasonably, "it certainly didn't possess much power. Look what happened to Buffalobeard Village."

The other raiders burst out laughing and gestured to the smoking lodges, but the big man didn't seem amused.

He pointed his atlatl at Screech Owl's gray head. "We've been gathering every Spirit object we can find. We want that Stone Wolf, and the girl who possesses it."

Screech Owl went rigid. "What girl?"

As though annoyed by the question, the raider gripped Screech Owl's shoulder and shoved him backward. Twig's mother covered her head, expecting a blow. "We have to find that Wolf. I know a little girl has it. Where is it? What have you done with it?"

Screech Owl tucked his hands into the folds of his shirt, but before he did, Greyhawk saw them shake. After a few moments, Screech Owl asked, "What do you want with all these Spirit objects?"

The big raider leaned down and grinned at Screech Owl with broken, yellow teeth. "Our chief, the Blessed Nightcrow, has foreseen the destruction of our world. In his vision, a giant ball of light sets the forests on fire, the Ice Giants turn black, and war breaks out. He's going to use the power in the Spirit objects to kill all of you before you can attack us in the scramble for what is left of the food."

"Really? Does he know how to extract the power? That's not as easy as it sounds. Believe me, I know. Is Nightcrow that powerful?"

"He is the Thornback People's most powerful Spirit dreamer. And once he has stolen all the sacred objects from his enemies, he will be the most powerful dreamer in the world."

"And the girl? Why does he need her?" Screech Owl asked.

Hook shrugged. "He does. That is all I know, or need to know. She must be very power—"

A hoarse shout rent the night, and Greyhawk almost screamed he was so frightened by it. He desperately peered through the rocks to see what was happening.

Near the eastern ridge on the far side of the village, one of the raiders pulled a child and a man from the darkness and dragged them into the glow of the burning lodges.

"Stop it, let me go!" the boy shouted.

*Grizzly! It's Grizzly!*

The raider hauled Grizzly by the scruff of his neck while he twisted wildly, kicking, biting, trying to wrench free of the man's iron hands.

Grizzly's father, Black Star, had been wounded. He was dragging his right foot, and blood soaked his pant leg.

"Let me go!" Grizzly screamed and sank his teeth into the raider's hand.

"You little wildcat!" the raider shouted and lifted his war club to kill Grizzly.

Before he could land the blow, Black Star leaped upon the raider, and they toppled to the ground in a rolling, fighting blur. Both men roared at the tops of their lungs.

Three other raiders ran forward and began beating Black Star with their war clubs. It took less than ten heartbeats for Black Star to collapse on the ground.

Grizzly stood as though frozen in shock, staring at his father's brain, where it was visible through the crack in his skull.

The raider who had threatened Grizzly got to his feet and lunged at Grizzly to finish the job and kill him.

The big raider shouted, "No, Chub! Wait. Bring him here."

"What for?"

"Because I said so!"

Chub lifted his war club, ready to strike Grizzly despite his war chief's orders. "He's a little animal, Hook. The sooner we kill him, the better!"

Another warrior, a very tall man, grabbed Grizzly and dragged him away from Chub, which obviously enraged Chub. He glared pure death at the insolent warrior.

"Here he is," the tall man said as he shoved Grizzly down at Hook's feet.

"Good work, Shrike," Hook praised and studied Grizzly. "Children are less skilled at lying. Perhaps he knows where the Stone Wolf is."

Grizzly scrambled to his knees, breathing hard, and stared at his dead father as though expecting him to rise.

"What's your name?" Hook demanded to know.

"Grizzly." His voice broke, and tears filled his eyes.

"Grizzly, what happened to the Stone Wolf?"

"Why don't you ask her?" Grizzly responded, pointing at Twig's mother. "Her name is Riddle. She's the keeper of the Wolf Bundle."

Hook didn't deign to glance at Screech Owl or Riddle. He motioned for Chub to step back and knelt before Grizzly, staring hard into his terrified eyes. "Which lodge belonged to Riddle?"

Grizzly thrust out his arm to show where it was.

Hook looked up, and Chub said, "We searched it. We found nothing valuable in the ashes."

Hook turned back to Grizzly. "Where could it be if it wasn't in her lodge?"

Grizzly stared at his dead father, and tears streamed down his face. "M-Maybe Twig has it."

Greyhawk thought he was going to throw up.

"Twig?" Hook almost shouted. He looked excited. "The girl's name is Twig? Where is she?"

"I don't know. I—I saw her run away."

Hook rose to his feet and ordered, "Spotted Skull, take five warriors. Tell our men they are hunting for a little girl. We'll finish the job here; then we'll join you in the search."

"Yes, Hook."

Greyhawk silently eased back into the shadows and, shaking badly, leaned against the cold rocks. Hook was splitting his forces. Greyhawk's father had told him a war chief should never do that unless he had a lot of warriors to spare. Greyhawk counted twenty-one Thornback raiders. With six gone, that left fifteen. If only his father were here...

Yipper stood up and nosed Greyhawk's arm. He didn't seem to be breathing, just waiting for a command.

Greyhawk let out a shaky breath. He had to find Twig before the raiders did. He'd known Twig all his life. He knew her favorite hiding places. He could find her—but how could he get away and start looking without the raiders seeing him?

Greyhawk motioned for Yipper to follow and crawled along in the shadows of the boulders with Yipper at his heels. Pure black, Yipper blended with the darkness.

When Greyhawk had only ten paces left to reach the eastern ridge, he saw the gap in the defensive wall. He had to cross there, but he would be in full view of the raiders if he did.

"Oh, Yipper," he whispered. "We're in trouble."

Yipper cocked his ears. He knew that tone of voice; it meant he should be afraid, and he understood perfectly. He went stone still.

Greyhawk got down flat on his stomach and motioned for Yipper to do the same. Side by side, they slid across the ground on their bellies until they reached the gap. It was about as long as Greyhawk was tall. If he could just...

*"Did you think you could escape?"* a man roared from behind him.

Greyhawk spun around. The raider had his war club up, ready to swing it at Greyhawk's head.

Greyhawk opened his mouth to scream just as Yipper sprang out of the darkness, knocked the raider to the ground, and leaped for the man's throat. When he clamped his powerful jaws around the man's neck, a horrifying blend of snarls and screams erupted.

Greyhawk lunged into the darkness and ran with all his might.

Hook spun and shouted, "Netsink?"

Two warriors charged out to help their friend, and the sounds of clubs striking flesh rose. Yipper's snarls turned into shrieks of pain, then suddenly stopped.

Hook must have seen Greyhawk. He shouted, *"There's a boy! Catch him!"*

# twelve

The moonlight was bright enough that every pebble cast a shadow across the tundra.

Which didn't help Greyhawk where he hid in the crevice in the rocks. Every time he even thought about crawling out and running, he was clearly visible.

Twenty paces away, two raiders searched the rocks for him. Both men carried quivers filled with spears over their shoulders and atlatls in their hands.

"I saw the brat come this way," the tall warrior said. As he moved, he was little more than a black shape.

"Maybe, but we're never going to find him in the darkness, Copper Falcon," the shorter man replied. "We've been blundering around for three hands of time. We should wait until morning and then track him down. He's a boy. We'll catch him quick once we can see his tracks."

Copper Falcon stopped and stretched his tired back muscles. "Yes, and if I were war chief, that is the order I would have given. But I am only Hook's deputy. I can't disobey his orders, and he ordered us to catch the boy. So we keep hunting."

The short man flapped his arms in irritation. "But we're accomplishing nothing. We're probably just getting farther and farther from the boy's trail. When dawn comes, we'll have to go right back to the village and start over again at the place where his trail begins."

"Well, if we have to go back, at least we'll be able to steal something for our trouble."

Catfish heaved an annoyed sigh. "I wish we'd been assigned to the party hunting for the girl. If we could get our hands on that Stone Wolf first, we'd be heroes."

"I've been thinking about that."

"You have?"

"Of course." Copper Falcon continued in a low voice, as though he feared someone might overhear him, "If we could get our hands on that Wolf, we could run straight home and personally present it to Chief Nightcrow. He would be very grateful."

"Maybe grateful enough to make you war chief?"

Copper Falcon smiled, and his teeth glinted in the moonlight. "Maybe."

Catfish chuckled. "You are an ambitious man, did you know that? Don't forget that Shrike will object. He's been one of Hook's deputies longer than you have."

"I'm not greedy, just hungry for power that

should have been mine two summers ago. I don't know why Nightcrow picked Hook over me, but it was an idiotic choice. As for Shrike, he'll have to fight me for the right."

Catfish lowered a hand to his belly and rubbed it. "Speaking of hunger, I'm hungry, too, but not for power. We haven't eaten since yesterday morning. I'm starving, aren't you?"

Copper Falcon nodded. "My stomach is so empty it feels like a hole goes all the way through me."

Copper Falcon walked to the crest of the ridge and peered down across the starlit tundra. A short distance away, a giant sloth, the size of a buffalo, snuffled the tundra while it used its huge claws to dig for roots. Covered with coarse, shaggy hair, the slow-moving animal made an easy target for supper.

Copper Falcon said, "Let's kill that sloth and fill our bellies before we continue. We'll both be happier."

"Now you're making sense." The short warrior drew a spear from his quiver and nocked it in his atlatl.

They both crept out of the rocks and began circling around, hunting the sloth.

Greyhawk waited until all of their attention was focused on the sloth, then he edged out of the rocks and sneaked away, heading in the opposite direction.

# thirteen

As night deepened, the rumbling moans of the Ice Giants grew so loud the ground quaked beneath Twig's feet. She shivered and tried to stop crying. For most of the night, she'd lain curled on her side in this willow thicket, with her head pillowed on her arm, watching the trails below. Moon Maiden cast a silver glow over the night.

"Oh, Screech Owl. Where are you? Are you coming to find me?"

Maybe he was dead. Maybe they were all dead, and she was alone.

Twig covered her mouth with her hands and sobbed. All her life, whenever Mother had shouted at her, she'd come to hide in this thicket until the hurt went away. Tonight, she would have given anything to know her mother was alive and angry with her at home in their lodge.

"Mother. Please be alive, please."

She tucked the edges of Screech Owl's green shirt around her toes. Her teeth had been chattering all night. She was tired...so very tired. It took great effort to stay awake, to keep watch on the trails.

"Eagle-Man!" she called desperately to her Spirit Helper. "Help me stay awake. I have to wait for Screech Owl or Mother. They might not see me here. I have to stay awake."

Her voice faded as though the wind had sucked it away and blown it up to the Star People. Twig fought the heaviness of her eyes, but weariness overcame her, and sleep finally numbed her body and began to coil around her thoughts.

She was almost asleep when a sudden spot of warmth grew in the middle of her chest, the place where the Stone Wolf rested.

Faintly, a voice whispered, *No one wants to be a dreamer, Twig. But someone must be..."*

The hiss of a moccasin against stone brought Twig scrambling up in the darkness, crying, "Who— who's there?"

"Twig? Twig, it's me!" Greyhawk slowly made his way through the willows and crouched beside her. His black hair was filled with sticks and old leaves, as though he'd been crawling through brush all night.

"Greyhawk," she panted. "Where did you come from? I'm so glad to see you."

"I've been searching for you since the attack. We have to get out of here. There are raiders right behind me, and they're searching for both of us."

She rubbed the back of her neck, trying to wake up. "What do you mean...both of us?"

"The raiders are after you and the Stone Wolf. They won't give up until they find you."

Twig rose to her feet. Her knees were knocking. "Why do they think I have it?"

"It's a long story I'll tell you as we run."

Twig blinked. "Where's Yipper?"

Greyhawk's eyes filled with tears. "I—I don't know. He may be dead. He tried to protect me when a raider found me."

"The raiders found you?"

"Yes, just outside the village. A big man was going to club me, and Yipper jumped on him and knocked him down. I—I ran." A sob caught in his throat. He looked away. "I should have stayed, Twig! I shouldn't have left Yipper to fight the warriors alone!"

Grief made Twig's entire chest ache, but she put a hand on his shoulder. "Greyhawk, look at me." He swallowed hard and turned to face her. "Yipper wanted you to run. He was trying to give you time to get away. And he did. You're alive because of him. That's what he wanted. He loved you."

Tears silently ran down his cheeks. "I know."

"Besides...I'm sure he got away. He's probably sniffing out your trail right now."

Hope slackened Greyhawk's face. "Do you think so? Really?"

"Yes. You know how fast he is. He can outrun the wind."

Greyhawk blinked back his tears. "He is fast. Do

you remember that time he outran the pack of wolves that were chasing him?"

"I remember. Compared to wolves, outrunning warriors would have been easy. He got away, Greyhawk. He's alive."

That seemed to make him feel better. Greyhawk wiped his eyes on his sleeve and swallowed hard. He looked around at the night before he asked, "Twig, where should we go? We have to find a place to hide!"

"We can't hide. We have to go west."

"West? Why?"

She turned to stare at the shining slope of ice that ran down to meet the land in the distance. "Because that's where Cobia's cave is."

Wild with fear, Greyhawk hissed, "Twig, we can't go after Cobia! Our village was just attacked! We have to find a place to hide, and then we have to find our families to make sure they're all right!"

Twig took a moment to steady her nerves before she said, "Greyhawk, I—I think my dream is coming true. The attack on our village...I saw the flaming spears days ago. If my dream is coming true, we *must* find Cobia. Every Spirit Helper I've ever talked to told me that she's the only one who can truly save our families."

"But the raiders will track us!"

Twig shivered violently before she managed to control it. "Greyhawk? How long will it take us to get to Cobia's cave?"

"I don't know for sure. Puffer said that if she left early in the morning, she would be back to

Buffalobeard Village by nightfall—if her scouting party ran the entire way."

"That means it will probably take us around twenty-four hands of time. We can go hungry for that long, and we can eat ice for water. We can do this, Greyhawk. Come on."

One step at a time, she forced her feet to walk toward the lakeshore trail.

Greyhawk glanced around at the darkness before he ran to follow her.

# fourteen

Screech Owl sat beside Riddle, watching the ten raiders that Hook had left to "finish the job." The men were taking turns smacking the wounded in the heads with their war clubs while they searched the smoking lodges, stealing anything of value they could find. Chub trotted back with a polished conch shell necklace that had belonged to Chief Gill's wife. The shell had been traded from the far southern ocean. It was rare and beautiful.

"Look what I found!" he announced and grinned as he held it up.

The tall warrior, Shrike, reached out and ripped it from his fist. "Very nice. I appreciate the gift." He slipped the necklace over his head and chuckled at the surprised expression on Chub's face.

Chub shouted, "That's mine! Give it back, or I'll bash your brains out." He reached for his war club, but not fast enough.

Shrike lashed out with his atlatl, slammed it into

Chub's hand, and bone snapped loudly as the raider dropped to his knees, yelling in pain. Chub's left thumb stuck out at an odd angle.

"You broke my hand!" he shouted at Shrike.

Shrike laughed. "Get up. Let's kill these prisoners and go find War Chief Hook. He's probably already captured the girl and is headed home. Besides, we've stolen enough to last us moons."

Screech Owl bent down and whispered in Riddle's ear, "Get ready to run."

Her eyes went wide. "What are you going to do?"

"Try to stall them long enough for you and the others to get away."

As he started to stand, Riddle grabbed his arm and hissed, "No, Screech Owl, don't—"

Shrike said, "What are you doing, old man? Sit down!"

Screech Owl grinned. "Well, I will if you want me to, but I think I know where the Stone Wolf is hidden." He cautiously lifted a hand to point to the rocky ridge east of the village. "There's a little hollow where Chief Gill used to hide precious things."

Shrike turned to look at the ridge, and Screech Owl readied himself to leap but hesitated when he glimpsed movement among the rocks. There was something out there. Maybe...

Shrill war cries erupted from the rocks, and Elder Halfmoon charged out, wildly swinging his war club as though he couldn't quite see the raiders. Fifteen warriors followed him, including Searobin, who shouted at the captives, "Go on, run! Run!"

The captives went crazy. Women grabbed children by the hands, careened to their feet, and dashed away into the darkness while Screech Owl and the other men leaped for discarded spears and raced to join the fight.

# fifteen

Twig and Greyhawk watched Father Sun's crimson face rise over the Ice Giants. The ice and snow blazed, turning from pink to a brilliant orange as the ball of the sun slipped above the horizon. They had walked a long way during the night. Here, at this place, hundreds of black caves honeycombed the ice.

Greyhawk breathed, "Elder Halfmoon says that these caves twist back into the ice forever. He once tried to follow out the tunnels to find Cobia, but he got lost over and over again. Many of the tunnels connect far back in the ice, but there are lots of dead ends."

"He never found Cobia?" Twig asked.

Greyhawk shook his head.

Twig said, "No wonder he didn't want to take me. His eyes are even worse today. He was probably afraid of getting lost and never being able to find his way out again."

Greyhawk looked around. "Do you remember Elder Halfmoon telling Puffer that she would have to pass Oak-beam Village to find Hoarfrost Canyon?"

"Yes. But I don't know how to get there. Do you?"

Greyhawk studied the land. "Maybe."

Twig followed his gaze. To the west, the Ice Giants rose like shining blue-white cliffs. They'd been squealing and groaning even more than usual. It was as though they knew something she didn't and were trying to warn her.

"We should try to find Oakbeam Village first," she said.

Greyhawk frowned; then he pointed with his atlatl. "Oakbeam Village is that way. I think. But I'm telling you, we should *not* go there! We should go back and find our families first. If we just had my father here, and your grandfather, we could find her cave, and everything would be alright!"

With a confidence she didn't feel, Twig pulled her shoulders back and said, "I'm older than you, Greyhawk. I know what's best for us. I promise I'm not leading you to your death."

A hard swallow went down Greyhawk's throat. "Why did you say that? Did you dream my death? Or...our deaths?"

"Do you think I'd be leading us out here if I thought we were both going to die?"

Greyhawk glowered at her as though he feared she might...but when she started walking, he followed her down to the trail that skirted the ice caves.

Silver veils of fog blew in off the lake. They clutched at her with cold, transparent fingers.

Twig filled her lungs with the scents of water and damp earth, and when she exhaled, her breath frosted in the morning air. She saw nothing now, except fog. But the Stone Wolf resting over her heart had grown warm and heavy. Its weight seemed to be pulling her forward.

She stopped and stared down at the Wolf.

Greyhawk asked, "What are you staring at?"

"The Wolf. It's getting heavier and heavier. I swear it feels like a lump of granite ten times this size." She pulled the Wolf from her shirt. "Feel this."

Greyhawk reached out and grabbed the Wolf by the thong. The Wolf swung just beneath his fingers. "It *is* heavy! Why?"

"I...I think it knows how to find Cobia."

He dropped the Wolf and backed away, but his eyes remained glued to the shining obsidian Wolf. "What makes you think that?"

"The weight of the stone is tugging at my neck, pulling me along."

"Pulling you?"

"Yes, pulling me west."

Greyhawk looked to the west, toward the massive glaciers that glittered as though sprinkled with Stardust. "Toward Oakbeam Village?"

"I think so." She rubbed the back of her neck

where it hurt. The Wolf had grown so heavy that the thong was cutting into her skin.

Greyhawk asked, "Do you want me to carry it for a while?"

"No, I think that right now I need to. But thanks for offering. If it gets too heavy, I'll let you."

Whispering, he asked, "Has it talked to you?"

She put her hand over the Wolf. It warmed her cold fingers. "No, it's been very quiet. I don't think it needs to tell me where we're going. It's showing me the path."

He glanced at the Stone Wolf again. "Then you should lead."

Twig nodded and led the way out into a field of eerie ice pillars ten times the height of a man and half as wide. There were hundreds of them. As they moved between them, following the streams of water that cut twisting trails around the pillars, she felt like she was walking through a forest of tree trunks made of solid ice. Carved by the wind and water, some of the pillars seemed to have sculpted faces. The tallest pillar to her right was speckled with gravel and coated with windblown dirt. When Twig looked at the top, she swore she saw a straggly mop of hair and a man's twisted face, his mouth open in a hideous cry.

She shuddered. "I don't like this place, Grey-hawk. Let's hurry and get through it."

Greyhawk was looking around as though he felt it too—that strange sensation that they were being watched by something not quite human. "I'm hurry-ing," he said.

They weaved through the forest of pillars, moving so fast that when they entered the narrow ice canyon, barely two body-lengths wide, they almost stumbled over the first human skeleton.

"Twig!" Greyhawk shouted as he stopped dead in his tracks.

She bumped into him, breathing hard.

The mangled bodies had long since been eaten. Only the bones remained, adorned with shreds of clothing that were scattered among the pillars, along with several discarded weapons.

Twig asked, "Who are they?"

Greyhawk's eyes focused instantly on an atlatl, and he ran to pick it up. Red, black, and white designs encircled the shaft. "I think this is War Chief Puffer's atlatl."

"Are you sure?"

"Yes." She was my clan, Smoky Shrew Clan. I used to watch her practice all day long, hoping that one day I could cast my spear as far as she could. I swear this is hers."

Twig said, "Then..this is our war party?"

"It must be."

Greyhawk wandered around for a while, collecting spears while he studied the tracks that marked the snow, both human and animal. Finally, he said, "A bear's been at them. That's why the bones are broken and scattered everywhere."

"This must be where they were ambushed."

"Yes." He stared at Twig, and fear lit his eyes. "If we're smart, we'll get out of here before anyone has a chance to ambush us."

Twig grabbed a spear from the ground and sprinted up the trail. In the distance, she could see the lake again, shining blue, though the shore was still mounded with boulders and dirty ice.

When they rounded the next bend, they left the ice pillars behind, but a low ridge of boulders snaked along the ground to the right. They slowed down, feeling relieved to be out of the strange pillars.

Until they heard a snuffle.

Twig's heart thundered when Grandfather Brown Bear lumbered from behind a boulder and onto the trail in front of them.

"Oh, no," Twig gasped and stumbled backward.

The bear saw them and stood on his hind legs to sniff the breeze. The wind was blowing right up their backs, blowing their scents to him. He was three times their height, and when he dropped to all fours again, his massive head seemed too big to be real. A low growl came up the bear's throat.

"He's getting ready to charge," Greyhawk said.

Twig felt faint.

Greyhawk grabbed her by the back of the coat and dragged her behind a boulder.

"Greyhawk," she said in a voice that sounded too high-pitched to be her own voice. "What are we—"

"Quiet!" Greyhawk leaned very close to her ear and whispered, "Follow me. I—I can do this. Father taught me how to do this. Stay close to me!"

# sixteen

Greyhawk bent low and sneaked around until he found a game trail that led up over the boulder ridge. "Twig, do what I do."

Twig bent low—as he had—and followed him up the trail. When they reached the top, Greyhawk peered over the edge at the bear thirty hands below them. The huge predator had his nose to the ground. He was tracking them. It wouldn't be long until he climbed right up the game trail and found them.

Greyhawk whispered to Twig, "We have to circle around to get upwind from the bear so he can't smell us."

"Do you think we can shake him?"

"I don't know, but if he finds us, don't run. He's much faster than we are. He'll have us down with our heads ripped off in a few heartbeats. Start looking for a place to hide. A place deep enough that he can't reach in with his paw and pull us out."

Twig spun around, searched the rocks, and pointed. "What about that rock shelter? Is it big enough for both of us?"

They ran to look. The shelter, made from three boulders that had toppled together, was deep but narrow. They'd have to crawl in on their bellies and lie flat.

"You go in, Twig. I'm going to wait to see if the bear is still following us."

As Twig slid beneath the boulders and into the darkness, she said, "Come on, Greyhawk. It's big enough for both of us."

He answered, "Push as far back as you can so I'll have space."

Greyhawk knelt and watched Twig slide to the very back of the shelter with her spear clutched in her fist. It was just as he'd suspected. The rock shelter wasn't deep enough for two of them to hide out of the bear's reach. If he crawled in there with her, the bear would just reach in, sink his claws into Greyhawk's flesh, and pull him out.

He rose on shaky legs and wilted against the boulder, trying to force himself to think. He had to remember every lesson he'd ever learned. He glanced down at his atlatl and four spears. His aim was pretty good, but he wasn't very strong. He'd have to get dangerously close to the bear.

He scanned the ridgetop. He could hear his father's voice echoing in his head: *How can you use the landscape to help you with your hunt?* A plan was forming somewhere inside him; he could see how the hunt might play out *if* he did everything right.

Greyhawk trotted to the opposite side of the trail and climbed up to the highest point in the boulders, twenty hands above the trail. The rock shelter where Twig hid was directly across from him.

Greyhawk nocked a spear in his atlatl and hunkered down in the rocks.

"Be Mountain Lion," he whispered to himself. "Watch. Wait."

*You choose when to strike. Never let the enemy make the first move. But if he attacks before you're ready, you must—*

The bear came up the trail. His massive shoulders rolled as he walked, sniffing out their trail with ease. Though he was a brown bear, his hair was tipped with silver, giving it a shimmer.

The bear suddenly lifted its huge head and scented the wind; then his gaze went directly to the rock shelter where Twig hid.

The bear snuffled as he lumbered toward it.

Greyhawk's throat went tight. He gripped his nocked atlatl hard, but his hand was shaking badly. Would he be able to cast accurately? He checked to make certain his other three spears were within reach.

The bear lowered his head and stared into the shelter. Twig didn't make a sound. The bear growled, and a white cloud of breath drifted away on the cold wind.

Greyhawk could imagine Twig lying inside, staring right into the shining eyes of the bear.

The bear reached into the shelter with his paw to find Twig. When he couldn't reach her, he got down on his belly and extended his arm as far as he could, trying to claw her out.

He must have come close. Twig let out a small cry of shock, which made the bear even more determined. He growled ferociously and scrambled around to stuff both paws and as much of his head as he could into the opening. In the process, he turned sideways.

Greyhawk rose on trembling legs and focused all of his attention on the place right behind the bear's shoulder where the heart rested. He threw his spear with every ounce of strength in his panicked muscles. He cast so hard that the motion of the throw almost carried him over the edge of the boulders and sent him crashing down onto the trail beside the bear...but he caught himself just in time.

His spear sliced into the bear's side and went deep inside its chest. The bear roared and scrambled out of the rock shelter; then he spun around and around, ripping at the spear in his side, trying to tear it out.

Terrified and elated, Greyhawk forgot his father's most important lesson: *As soon as you cast, immediately nock another spear in your atlatl...*

He remembered only when the bear saw him, let out a blood-tingling roar, and charged.

Greyhawk reached for another spear and fumbled to get it nocked as the bear leaped up the boulders as though they were mere stepping stones. He cast again, missed, and quickly nocked another spear. In less than five heartbeats, Grandfather Brown Bear was standing right in front of Greyhawk, with bloody breath blowing from his nostrils and blood dripping from his side.

"Don't run, don't run, *don't run,*" Greyhawk hissed to himself as he drew back his atlatl and took aim.

"Grandfather," he prayed, "please, please, let me kill you. Our families are dying. We have to find Cobia."

Grandfather Brown Bear cocked his head, as though listening to Greyhawk's voice... Then he bounded forward with his huge jaws open to crush Greyhawk's skull.

Greyhawk cast his spear and, by instinct, threw himself aside, rolling away as the bear's strong jaws snapped for his leg. When the bear missed, he swiped out with a paw bigger than Greyhawk's head, and gleaming claws ripped into Greyhawk's left arm. The pain was so stunning that it left Greyhawk breathless.

Forgetting every lesson he knew, Greyhawk lunged to his feet and ran.

The bear was right behind him, roaring. The bloody spear in its front shoulder, Greyhawk's last cast, flopped with every bound.

When Greyhawk could feel Bear's hot breath on the back of his neck, he jumped headfirst over the edge of the ridge and tumbled down the slope like a thrown rock. His head bashed every boulder on the way down.

He landed facedown at the bottom, dazed. For a

moment, he didn't know where he was. He crawled to his hands and knees and looked around. He didn't recognize this place. Where was...

*"Greyhawk!"* Twig screamed.

He scrambled up to look at her.

Halfway down the slope, the bear had collapsed on his side; his strained breathing was like a tearing sound on the wind. Twig stood two paces away with a spear in her hand, ready if the bear stood up again.

"Are you all right?" Twig called.

"Yes," he said and climbed the slope, taking gulps of the cold air. Blood trickled down his face from his wounded head, and his arm burned as though afire. "At least I'm alive."

"Thank the Spirits," Twig said when he got close. "When I saw you at the bottom of the slope, I thought... You're bleeding! Are you hurt?" She ran to him.

Greyhawk sank down atop a rock five paces from the dying animal. Frozen puffs of breath still escaped the bear's jaws, but the soul was going out of his wide eyes. Greyhawk's first spear had gone true. It must have pierced the bear's heart.

Twig knelt by Greyhawk's side, looked at his head wounds, and pulled back the blood-soaked shreds of his shirt to examine his wound. Her pretty face tensed. "The bear's claws sliced deep, Greyhawk. I'm going to have to bandage this."

Greyhawk exhaled hard. His arm had started to hurt badly, and his muscles felt like boiled grass stems, but they had to keep going. He shoved to his feet. "Let's cut some strips of bear meat and get out of here, Twig. The raiders are still after us. I know they are."

"First, I need to bandage your arm. Stay here. I'll run back to the ambush site and collect some strips of clothing from our dead warriors. After I'm done, I'll cut the strips of meat, then we'll go."

He gratefully sat down again. His head had begun to throb. Through swimming eyes, he looked at the bear. Its legs trembled in sudden weakness, then pawed the air for a few moments before going still. Finally, his huge mouth lolled open, revealing sharp teeth longer than Greyhawk's hand.

Greyhawk's eyes silently traced the lines of Bear's huge body, noting his two spears. He had killed a bear. By the laws of his clan, he had just become a man.

If his father was alive, he would be proud.

# seventeen

By afternoon, they knew they were being hunted. Fresh tracks marked the muddy trail, both in front and behind them. Greyhawk knew because he'd sneaked back down the trail to check. There were two war parties searching for them.

He readjusted his bandaged arm. It hurt badly. If he'd been at home, he would have gone to Twig's mother, and she would have placed a willow-bark poultice on the wound. By now, the intense pain would have eased, and he'd be able to breathe. Instead, every time he filled his lungs, the gashes in his arm lanced him with fiery agony. He turned and gazed to the south. Just beyond the tundra, vast forests whiskered the land. He looked at them longingly. In the autumn, his village moved south to harvest the pecans, walnuts, and hazelnuts. He loved the forests best of all. Would he ever live there again?

"More tracks," Twig said.

Greyhawk turned and saw her kneel in the trail ahead. He walked up and crouched to examine the new moccasin prints. The Thornback People made their moccasins differently than the People of the Dawnland. The raiders' moccasins had a seam down the middle of the sole that left a clear imprint in the mud.

Twig nervously licked her lips. Wind Woman fluttered long black hair around her face. "What do you think? Should we go back? Maybe wait until tomorrow and find another trail?"

"No." Greyhawk rose to his feet, and his bandaged arm screamed in pain. He'd heard the big Thornback warrior's voice. His leader, Nightcrow, wanted the Stone Wolf and Twig. He had ordered his men to find them, no matter the cost. They wouldn't stop hunting Twig until they found her. "No, we keep going."

Fear glittered in Twig's eyes. "Are you sure?"

Softly, he said, "I'm scared, too, Twig. But I believe in your dream. We have to find Cobia. It's the only way to save our people."

"You mean, if any of them are still alive." A sob caught in her throat.

Greyhawk gripped his nocked atlatl in his right fist. She must be imagining the dead bodies of her mother, Screech Owl, and her grandfather, lying in the charred remains of their village.

He knew because every moment since he'd escaped, he'd been imagining the same thing. One instant, he saw his father alive and smiling at him, and the next instant, he saw his father sprawled facedown in the ashes of Buffalobeard Village. The worst images were of Yipper. If the raiders had killed him, they would have eaten him, and the only thing Greyhawk would find when he got home was Yipper's bones. The thought was almost too much to bear. Yipper had saved him, not just the night of the attack, but every day. He couldn't even remember a time when Yipper was not there beside him, as loyal as his own shadow, fighting for Greyhawk without ever asking for anything in return. Except maybe an occasional pat on the head or a scratch behind the ear. His throat tightened with grief.

He swallowed hard to push it away and said, "Some of our relatives lived, Twig."

"How do you know?"

"My father once told me that someone always lives through a battle. He said I should remember that, because when I went on my first battle-walk, the survivors would hate me and hunt me forever for killing their loved ones."

"Why did he tell you that?"

"He didn't want me to feel proud of killing. He told me it was always bad, just sometimes necessary to protect our people."

Twig dipped three handfuls of water from a puddle and drank them; then she stood up. "We're both tired. We should eat."

"We can't build a fire to cook, or the smoke will lead the raiders right to us."

"That's all right. Bear meat is good raw."

She reached into her belt pouch and drew out several strips of the rich red meat. She gave some to Greyhawk.

"Let's sit down," he said. "We should rest for as long as we can."

"Even with the raiders so close?"

"Yes, Twig. If we don't rest, we'll be too tired to think, and if we can't think, they *will* catch us."

She sat down, and he sat beside her. They chewed the meat in silence, both studying the trails, looking for their enemies.

The meat was tender and sweet. With each bite, Greyhawk felt strength flowing back into his exhausted body.

"I've been thinking about Cobia," Twig said.

Greyhawk looked at her. "So have I. Every spare moment, when I'm not afraid the raiders will kill us, I'm afraid she will."

Twig took another bite of meat and ate it. "I was wondering how I would feel if I'd watched my mother be killed, then been kidnapped and hauled far away to be raised by my enemies."

"I know how I'd feel. I'd hate them."

"Even if they'd been good to you? Even if you'd been kidnapped as a baby and your enemies were the only family you had ever known?"

Greyhawk considered that. "I guess if I didn't remember my real family, and my enemies loved me, I'd probably love them back."

"So would I." Twig started to eat another bite of meat but stopped. "At least until I found out the truth. Then I think I'd be lost and confused."

"Would you? I'd be scared."

"Why?"

"Because if they'd killed my family, they could kill me, too."

Twig propped her strip of bear meat on her knee and seemed to be watching the ice crystals that blew off the glaciers in the distance. The air sparkled.

"Do you think Cobia was scared? Is that why she left Buffalobeard Village?"

He shrugged. "Maybe."

Wind Woman gusted across the tundra and tugged at Greyhawk's shirt. He reached up to hold his collar closed while he ate his last bite of bear meat.

Twig finished eating and heaved a deep sigh. "Do you think we should try to sleep for a while?"

Greyhawk shoved to his feet and looked up and down the trail. He saw only a herd of buffalo grazing to the southwest and a few caribou scattered along the lakeshore.

"You try to sleep, Twig. I'll stand guard."

"But you're as tired as I am."

"We'll switch off. Next time, I'll sleep while you stand guard."

She thought about it for what seemed like a long time, then said, "Don't let me sleep for more than a quarter hand of time."

Greyhawk nodded, and Twig curled up on her side on the ground. She was so tired that she fell asleep almost immediately. He watched her face go from being taut and anxious to the peaceful relaxation of deep sleep.

Greyhawk walked a short distance away and climbed on top of a boulder. It was as tall as he was. He could see much farther from up here. He wished they could go back in time, to the days before...

The Ice Giants growled, and the ground shook. Out in the lake, a huge wall of ice broke away from the glacier and crashed into the water. A splash shot high into the air; then the iceberg dipped and rocked until it settled down. The other icebergs seemed afraid of the new one. They drifted away from it.

The ground shook harder, and the Ice Giants groaned loud enough and long enough to terrify him. He glanced down at Twig. She did not wake up.

Finally, the earthquake stopped, and Greyhawk brought up his knees and propped his injured arm on them, where it hurt a little less; then he concentrated on the trails. There were raiders out there, very close, looking everywhere for them. He had to pay attention.

Barely five hundred heartbeats later, he glimpsed black specks on the eastern trail.

Greyhawk flattened out on his belly and watched them. Were they animals? Or warriors?

Very soon, he knew the answer. The long spears they carried in their quivers swayed as they trotted.

He scrambled down off the boulder and ran for Twig. When he saw her, he whispered, "Twig? Twig, we have to go! There are raiders coming!"

She gasped and staggered to her feet, still half-asleep. "Go on! I'll follow you."

Greyhawk charged for the trail that led south into the forests.

# eighteen

If the raiders hadn't already seen them, they probably would the instant Greyhawk and Twig trotted to the high point in the trail, just ahead.

Greyhawk leaped over an ice-rimmed puddle and sprinted up and over the high spot, then hurled himself down the other side, getting out of sight as fast as he could.

Twig was right on his heels. He could hear her moccasins pounding the ground.

When they reached the low spot, Greyhawk dared to turn around and look. Twig's pretty face was flushed, and she was breathing hard.

"Are we safe?" she asked. "Did they see us?"

"Probably. We should act as if they did. Come on. If we run flat-out, we'll be to the trees in less than one-half hand of time."

When they entered the dark shadows of the forest, the temperature dropped, and their breath froze into white puffs. Snow glistened in the hollows.

Every wet scent of the forest smelled incredibly clear to Greyhawk, as if it had soaked into his body and was being carried through his veins. The sweetness of the pines mixed with the bitter tang of rotting oak leaves and the earthiness of melting snow.

"Greyhawk?" Twig called in a low voice. "Let's find a place to hide and wait to see if we're being followed."

"Let's get deeper into the forest first."

He found a game trail covered with deer tracks and trotted forward.

The deeper into the forest they ran, the taller and thicker the trees grew. He glanced up. High above, the branches of the freshly leafed-out oaks created a dense weave that blocked most of the sunlight, leaving the forest floor in shadow. Towering spruce and pine trees grew between the oaks; their tops seemed to pierce the clouds.

"I can't run anymore, Greyhawk," Twig panted. "Please, let's stop. Just for a little while."

"All right."

Cold wind gusted across his face as he looked around. A big pile of deadfall darkened the forest floor to his right. He veered off the trail and headed for it.

Over many tens of summers, trees had died and toppled over each other to form a tangled fortress of logs. Great crooked branches held the heavy trunks off the ground. Moss covered the smoke-colored bark. As he ducked low to examine the pile, it gave off a delicate fragrance. Animals had burrowed through the interior, creating a warren of tunnels. He saw wolf and bear droppings. A pure white snowshoe hare sat in the back, mostly hidden by the shadows, but his eyes gleamed.

Twig leaned over and said, "Can we hide here?"

"I think so. You go in and rest. I'll cover our tracks."

"No, I'll help you," she said and started to turn back.

"Please, Twig, it will be easier if I'm only covering my own tracks when I come back."

"Oh." She nodded. "You're right."

As Twig got down on her knees and crawled into the cold darkness, the hare shot away through the tunnels and disappeared.

Greyhawk grabbed a handful of old leaves and began backing up, brushing away their tracks as he went. When he reached the game trail, he stood up and examined it. They had left clear prints in the snow and mud.

If they were being followed, the raiders would be able to track them right to this pile of deadfall.

He adjusted his wounded arm. It ached as though afire.

His father's voice seeped into his thoughts: *When you can't erase your trail, Son, cover it with whatever you can find.*

Greyhawk bent down and began scooping up old leaves and pine needles and dropping them onto their tracks. He tried to make it look natural, as though the debris had blown across the trail, not been dropped intentionally. Would it fool trained warriors?

He didn't know, but he couldn't think of anything else to do.

After a quarter hand of time, he straightened up. He had reached the edge of the trees, where they'd entered the forest. Their tracks continued up the wet trail. He didn't see any raiders, but just in case...

Greyhawk carefully stepped beyond the leaves where he'd covered their trail, then placed his feet into the last of his tracks and trotted off to the east, leaving a new trail for any pursuers to follow.

He skirted the edge of the forest, walked on fallen logs when he could, and climbed over rocks. If they were in a hurry, they wouldn't have time to backtrack him, and he hoped they would lose his trail altogether.

One thing he couldn't fake, however, and something they were sure to notice: two sets of tracks, his and Twig's, had made it to the edge of the trees, but only one set continued on. They would know that one of the children was hiding.

"Yes, but they're tired, too. I bet they'll take the easy way and chase after me rather than go thrashing through the forest looking for Twig."

Greyhawk tiptoed across a narrow line of rocks and stepped into a trickle of water that flowed down another game trail. It would wash away his tracks in no time. But it was very cold!

Twenty paces ahead, a tall pine tree grew alongside the trail. The lower dead branches had been broken off by the animals that used the trail. They made a perfect ladder.

Greyhawk reached the tree and climbed it. He sat on a thick branch thirty hands off the ground and looked out across the land.

It didn't take long. He saw the two search parties run together at the fork in the trail. They stood talking for less than one hundred heartbeats and loped toward the forest.

"They found our trail."

His legs were shaking as he climbed down and jumped onto a fallen log.

For too long, he stood there panting like a hunted animal, trying to decide what to do.

There were two search parties now. He hadn't anticipated they would join up. It meant that the war chief would have the luxury of sending one group of warriors to track him down and one to search for Twig.

The false trail he'd laid would slow them down... but it wouldn't stop them, not when they were this close.

He and Twig were going to have to make a run for it and pray they reached Cobia's cave before the raiders caught them.

With every ounce of strength he had left, he charged back through the forest for Twig.

War Chief Hook stopped at the edge of the trees and examined the tracks. The other warriors gathered around him, murmuring as they pondered the situation.

The children's trail had been obvious, until now.

As he thought, Hook rubbed his square jaw. "Two children came in, but only one child—probably the boy from the size of the foot—veered off. So..." He looked up and scanned the forest. Dark shadows cloaked the interior. "The other child, the girl, is hiding."

Copper Falcon, his deputy, propped his hands on his hips. Sticky patches of blood splattered his black war shirt. He had his long black hair tied back with a cord. "Shall I pursue the boy or the girl?"

Hook considered. "Take ten warriors and follow the boy. I'll take the rest of our force and find the girl. Meet me back here in one hand of time."

Copper Falcon bowed at the waist. "Yes, War Chief."

As Copper Falcon went about selecting the warriors for his search party, Hook examined the ground. Water dripped from the tree branches and filled every hollow, including the leaf-covered game trail. He knelt. Before her trail disappeared, the toes of the girl's moccasins had been pointed straight onto the game trail. He carefully began removing leaves, one at a time, until he saw the covered tracks.

He smiled to himself. The boy had done a good job. One day, if he lived, he would make a fine warrior.

Unfortunately, it was Hook's job to make sure the boy did not live.

He rose to his feet, held up a fist to indicate silence, and motioned for his warriors to fan out on either side of the hidden game trail.

The boy's skill would cost them time. They would have to go slowly and carefully if they wanted to find the girl.

But, in the end, they would find both children.

# nineteen

All day long, they'd been hiding and running. Twig was so exhausted, she felt light-headed. And Greyhawk looked pale and hurt. The pain in his wounded arm must be unbearable.

But at nightfall, Twig and Greyhawk found Oakbeam Village.

Empty. Burned to the ground.

"When did this happen?" she softly asked. "Can you tell?"

"Not long ago. Maybe yesterday."

Fog blew through the smoldering husks of lodges. Everywhere, wooden bowls and baskets tumbled in the wind. Many of the bodies lay just in front of burned lodges, as though the people had been killed the moment they'd ducked outside.

Twig felt suddenly cold. Her clan, the Blue Bear Clan, believed that the souls of the dead stayed in the village for three days before traveling to the

Land of the Dead. Twig could feel them. Each time a burned lodge pole creaked in the wind, she thought she heard voices.

Greyhawk kicked at a broken atlatl. Then he picked up two spears that must have missed their targets and been forgotten in the raging battle.

"Where are their families?" Greyhawk asked. "They should have come back to bury the bodies."

"Maybe they're all dead."

They followed the trail through the smoke-blackened chaos and westward around the edges of the ice flow, where the fog was especially thick. It was like walking through a shimmering white blanket. Here, at this place, the glaciers flowed down and spread out across the land to form towering ice cliffs cut by deep cracks and fissures and then honeycombed with tunnels that seemed to go back into the ice forever.

"What's that?" Twig said and blinked at the canyon that appeared and disappeared as the fog shifted.

Greyhawk stopped. "I—I don't know. Do you think it's Hoarfrost Canyon?"

The sheer walls rose fifty times their height, as though the frozen waste had been split by a lightning bolt cast by Earthmaker himself.

Twig clenched her fists to keep them from trembling. "Grandfather said that the entry to Cobia's cave was at the end of Hoarfrost Canyon. Sh-should we go look?"

Greyhawk nocked a spear in Puffer's atlatl. "Yes."

Twig exhaled a long, frightened breath and walked out onto the sand and gravel that filled the bottom of the canyon.

The deeper they went, the more the canyon narrowed, as though it were funneling them in to some unknown darkness, and the walls grew steeper and taller. Twig glanced up. In less than two hundred paces, the ice cliffs had soared to one hundred times their height. Caves and tunnels of every size and shape sank into the walls. Twig tried not to look inside them, for fear of what she might see looking back.

The canyon was quiet and still. Twig stopped.

"What's the matter with you?" Greyhawk asked.

"Power is loose. Can't you feel it?"

Greyhawk looked at the birds darting over the high ice walls and said, "No. But I believe you."

"Oh, Greyhawk, I wish Mother was here, or Screech Owl."

"Well, they're not. We have to do this by ourselves."

Twig stopped, and the Stone Wolf radiated warmth against her chest, tugging her deeper into the canyon. "I—I'm going, Wolf," she murmured.

As they kept walking, the ice above them knitted into a roof, and the canyon became a deep, dark tunnel. The huge black maw gaped as though ready to swallow them.

"Don't tell me we have to go deeper into this tunnel," Greyhawk hissed. "We don't have a torch. How will we see?"

"I don't know, I—"

Twig gasped when black flits of cloth darted from the caves to her right and flew straight at them. All she could do was stare at the glowing eyes in their soot-covered faces.

Greyhawk cried, *"Thornback raiders! Run, Twig!"* and he cast his spear. *"I said, RUN!"*

Twig ran. But she'd barely taken four steps when a man tackled her from behind and knocked her to the ground. She smashed her head on a rock. The world started to spin. Above her, she saw the grinning face of the raider, then glimpsed Greyhawk racing toward her with his atlatl up. He cast his spear, and the big raider let out a cry, leaped up, and ran away with Greyhawk's spear sticking from his chest. Greyhawk cast two more spears but missed.

Pain was swelling behind Twig's eyes like an enormous black bubble. She struggled to get to her feet but kept falling back to the ground.

The next thing she knew, Greyhawk had grabbed her and was crawling, dragging her by the hand, into a narrow ice tunnel barely wide enough for a child's body to pass through. Inside, the ice had a strange shimmer. Greyhawk stretched out flat on his belly and pulled her deeper into the darkness. Twig tried to crane her neck to see how far back the tunnel ran, but it was black ahead. Utterly black. After dragging Twig about twenty paces, the tunnel grew wide enough for Greyhawk to sit up. He stopped and released her hand. Twig lifted her head to look back down the tunnel into the gray light of dusk.

A big raider tried to squeeze into the opening,

but his shoulders were too wide. He cursed and backed out.

"Twig? Your head is bleeding. How badly are you hurt? *Answer me!*"

But she couldn't because the world was spinning into darkness, spinning...and she felt so sick.

# twenty

Shaking, greyhawk sat beside Twig and studied her face. Her eyes were sunken in twin black circles, and her breathing was ragged. "Are you all right, Twig?"

She winced as she turned her head for him, and in the faint light that penetrated the cave, he saw a mat of gore and blood.

"Oh, Twig," he whispered. "You have a bad head wound."

She stammered, "H-how long do we...how long before..."

"Before they find a way to reach us?"

She nodded. It was obviously hard for her to speak.

"I don't know, Twig."

Twenty paces away, outside, the raiders shouted. Several more smaller men tried to crawl into the opening but failed.

Greyhawk leaned back against the ice wall and

let out a breath. His wounded arm was bleeding again. The tunnel continued to his right, utterly dark. He had no idea how far back into the ice it went; it might be a dead-end. But for the moment, they were safe.

"Greyhawk?"

"Yes?"

She looked at him with frightened eyes. "We're t-trapped. We're never going to be able to find Cobia's cave from in here."

"I know," he said, feeling utterly defeated. Sweat was freezing on his face, and every nerve in his body screamed at him to run. But there was nowhere to go.

They had come so far, braved so many perils, and all of it for nothing. It made him ache deep down. Maybe they should have given up and gone back when she'd—

"So..." Twig took a deep breath and squinted her eyes as she said, "I'm going to try to dream my way there."

He jerked around, astonished. "Can you do that?"

Sheer terror strained her face. "I don't know. I— I feel sick, shaky. If I fall into the river at the edge of the Land of the Dead, I may not be strong enough to swim out."

"Then maybe you should wait. Tomorrow, when you're stronger, then you—"

"*Boy!*" one of the raiders shouted into the tunnel.

Greyhawk froze. They had built a fire outside, and he could see the man's shining face. He had a thick bandage around his throat, soaked with blood.

The raider said, "I just wanted you to know that I killed your filthy dog. I clubbed him until his head was mush, then I cut out his heart and ate it for supper."

Greyhawk couldn't speak. Sobs spasmed his chest. He wanted to shout *You're lying,* but he feared it was true. The last time he'd turned to look back, he'd seen two warriors running to help Netsink, and each had carried a war club.

Twig said, "Don't listen to him, Greyhawk. You know how fast Yipper is. He ran. He got away."

"Y-yes, I know he did."

But he didn't.

*"And you, girl!"* the raider called again. "Hook killed your mother, Riddle, and who was that old man with her? Shrike slit his throat clear through to his spine."

A strange numbness seemed to filter through Twig, as though her soul was loose and preparing to fly away. She kept opening her mouth, then closing it. Was she trying to speak?

Greyhawk slid closer to her. "He's lying. They're both alive, Twig. I know they are."

The raiders' shadows moved across the face of the cave. Twig whispered, "I have to try now, Grey-hawk. I have to try to dream."

"Can I help?"

She shook her head. "No. You're a warrior. I— I'm a dreamer."

With shaking hands, she tugged open the laces

on her belt pouch and pulled out the tiny spruce branch from First Woman's tree. It looked black in the dim light. She had tears running down her cheeks.

Greyhawk said, "You can do it, Twig. I know you can."

She closed her eyes.

In an agonized voice, she started calling, "Eagle-Man, Eagle-Man, Eagle-Man..."

# twenty-one

"Eagle Man, please, please, help me!" In the middle of the night, Twig was on the verge of giving up. Her throat was raw from calling out to her Spirit Helper, and the pain in her injured head had grown to fill the entire world.

She stopped for a moment and gulped in deep breaths of the icy air.

Greyhawk had positioned himself in front of her, between Twig and the raiders outside, but she could see around him. The raiders had built a fire in the mouth of the cave. They were melting it out, making it larger. The fire's gleam turned the inside of the tunnel a gaudy orange. It wouldn't be long before they'd enlarged the cave enough for a man to crawl in after them.

Twig curled on her side on the floor of the cave and choked out, "Eagle-Man, please, hear me? I need you. I can't do this without—"

The Ice Giants suddenly let out a low, deep-throated growl, and the ground shook.

And from somewhere far, far away, a voice called her name. It kept speaking, but she couldn't really understand what it was saying. She closed her eyes and tried to concentrate. Something about Cobia... finding Cobia...

Then the Stone Wolf grew hot against her chest, and she clearly heard a boy say, *"It's through here. This way. This is the way, Twig."*

*A* strange glitter danced behind her closed eyelids. Like a swarm of blue fireflies.

*"Twig?"* Greyhawk called, but she could barely hear him. "What's happening?"

It was as though Twig's soul had stepped out of her body.

She found herself walking down a dark ice tunnel, alone and scared. She couldn't feel her feet or hands, but her heart was beating. She could hear it.

She walked. And walked.

There were ice mountains, frozen creeks, and towering blue glaciers that leaned over her like monstrous beings.

After what seemed like days, the tunnel began to grow larger. She must be in the very heart of the Ice Giants, because their voices were deafeningly loud. The deeper she traveled, the larger the tunnel grew, until it became a shining blue cavern. There were ice spires everywhere, and she heard water lapping against a shore, as though a great ocean spread beneath the ice.

And...she thought she heard people chanting. The rhythm reminded her of the ghost chants her own people sang to drive away evil Spirits.

"Hello!" Twig shouted.

High-pitched squeals answered. They mixed with the chanting and echoed in a way that struck terror into Twig's heart.

"Hello! Who's there?"

The cavern seemed to close in around her, the ice walls bending down to peer at her more carefully. Twig shivered. This place was not beautiful, though she had the feeling that it was old, very old, and that living humans had never dared to tiptoe beyond the well-worn trails. To her left, tumbled piles of ice choked the floor, and wherever the blue light touched, the ice seemed alive, pulsing.

Twig turned around in a full circle. "Oh, Cobia, where are you? I'm scared. I don't know how to find you. Cobia?"

Sobs clutched at her chest as she started to run again, dashing down a dip in the trail and up the other side.

The chanting grew louder, and life stirred the depths of the cavern. But Twig did not think she knew this kind of life. Feet pounded—heavy, thrashing angrily in a dance that shook the trail.

Twig ran like the wind. Shadows moved at the edges of the trail, some of them loping along beside her, keeping pace while they hissed their resentment at her presence.

"Cobia? Cobia, please!"

She rounded a bend, and one of the dancers

leaped at her. He didn't have any arms or legs, just enormous black eyes and a protruding mouth shaped from pink pipe-stone. Colorful feathers adorned the dancer's costume.

"What do you want?" Twig asked.

The dancer dodged into a shadow. But Twig saw others moving nearby. Their masks glinted as they floated between the ice spires.

Twig ran on, racing down a winding trail, slowing only when the trail vanished. She couldn't see it anywhere. Which way should she go?

She decided to run straight ahead. Thirty paces later, the tunnel narrowed. If it shrank any more, she would be crawling on her hands and knees.

Suddenly, she broke out of the tunnel and stepped into a huge washed-out cavern. High above her, Star People glittered. Trails led off in every direction. Ten or more!

Twig spun around, examining the path that dropped off down a long slope. Then she looked at the trail that climbed into another ice chamber above her.

From out of her memories, she heard a voice whisper, *"To step onto the path, you must leave it. Only the lost come to stand before the entrance to Cobia's cave."*

Tears blurred her eyes. She looked back down the trail. Even from this distance, she could see dark shapes moving. "But the only place without paths is that horrible cavern."

Twig clenched her fists, took a deep breath to fight her fear, and walked down, down through the small tunnel and into the cavern where there were no trails, where dark shadows watched in silence.

The chanting started again.

Twig shouted, "Eagle-Man?"

She waited.

For a while, she thought she might be all right.

Then, the masked dancers returned and floated around her like a ring of wolves. She couldn't see them clearly. Just flashes of hideous red mouths or of long beaks carved from pale wood. When she looked the hardest, the dancers vanished into twists of ice.

"Eagle-Man? Help me! Show me the way to Cobia's cave!"

The shadows went still. Twig jerked around, trying to figure out what they were doing. The strange chant had stopped, the cavern gone silent.

"Eagle-Man?"

Something glimmered to her right. It seemed a trick of starlight when the figure loomed up from the heart of the darkness and stepped toward her.

*"I heard you, Dreamer."*

Relief made Twig laugh. "Eagle-Man!" She ran to him, weaving between ice spires. "Thank you. I've been so lost, I—"

Eagle-Man lowered his head, and his beak opened, revealing sharp teeth. He shrieked like Hawk.

Then he spread his wings and dove at her.

# twenty-two

Twig screamed as she ran headlong through the piles of tumbled ice.

Eagle-Man's feet thumped the ground behind Twig as he danced his pursuit, spinning and leaping, his wings outspread so that the feathers brushed the ground. The blue gleam coated his body until each feather shimmered like liquid turquoise.

She tripped, stumbled into a rock, and caught her balance. Her knees were trembling.

Shadows flicked through the broken chunks of ice. Every so often, she caught sight of a mask, just a glimpse of jasper or shell beads.

Eagle-Man's steps echoed: thump-thump-thumpety-thump. Then they stopped.

Twig looked up and cried out in horror when she saw him perched on an icy ledge over her head. He had tucked in his wings and bent forward to peer down at her, like Vulture, waiting for a wounded deer to die. His snakeskin belly glittered.

"Why are you hunting me?" Twig cried. "You are my Spirit Helper!"

"Yes," Eagle-Man hissed, sounding like a snake, "I am." His black eyes gleamed as he shifted on the ledge, stepping back and forth in a strange dance. Gravel cascaded from the ledge with each stamp of his feet.

Movement stirred the shadows, and six ghostly forms shuffled out from the narrow tunnel. Some wore bushy-headed masks of beautifully woven grass; others had animal masks decorated with the upcurving horns of buffalo. The seashells on their leggings blazed in the light. Through the enormous sockets of their eyes, only blackness showed: empty, ominous, with no glint of life.

They closed in around her and began throwing spruce pollen at her. It netted her hair and stuck to her arms and legs.

"What are you doing?"

Spruce pollen purified and sanctified the way for power. But she did not understand why they were throwing it on her.

Finally, the dancers shuffled backward and opened their hands to Eagle-Man, who was circling near the cavern ceiling. He looked like a black dot.

*"Will you give up, Twig? Or will you fly for your people?"*

*"I* want to fly, Eagle-Man! I've always wanted to!"

Eagle-Man let out a cry of triumph and plummeted down, his sharp talons reaching for her.

Twig shrieked when he knocked her to the ground and clamped his talons around her chest in the manner of Eagle catching Chipmunk.

"Eagle-Man, no! You're my Spirit...Helper." She coughed as the air went out of her lungs in a gush. Her arms and legs flailed weakly while his talons tightened, and she could hear her ribs cracking.

The chanting began again.

Eagle-Man lowered his head and stared into Twig's terrified eyes.

*"This is the moment Screech Owl told you about. The moment when you must step into the mouth of the Spirit that wants to chew you up. Are you brave enough, Twig?"*

A gray haze fluttered at the edge of Twig's vision.

In a bare whisper, she said, "Yes."

With a wrench, Eagle-Man sank his claws deeper into her flesh, and his huge beak dropped out of the gray to tear at her chest and arms. She felt her flesh being torn from her bones as he devoured her.

Twig gave a final gasp as Eagle-Man's beak opened and plunged for her eyes. The last of her body began sliding down his throat, into his stomach.

Then...darkness.

# twenty-three

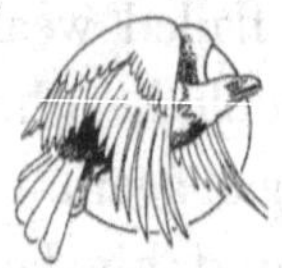

As though in a dream, Twig sank into the pool of blood, and it began to sway, rocking her back and forth. Her soul grew thinner and thinner, blending with the blood until it melted into the blackness. And from that nothingness came light. As though Eagle-Man had opened his beak, a stream of gold flooded down through an opening above. Twig reached for the warmth, but her fingers were...different...like, yes, like wings. Frail dreamer's wings strengthening, growing. She shook herself, and white bits of down fell away, revealing brown-speckled feathers.

From deep in her throat, Prairie Falcon's shriek rose: *kree, kree, kree!*

Twig spread her wings and soared upward toward the opening, where she flew out into a vast blue sky. Cloud People twisted and tumbled in the high winds. Twig tested her wings, diving and sailing on the cold air currents, feeling the way that each feather affected her flight when she flapped or tilted her tail. Joy brought tears to her eyes. Such freedom!

As she glided over the Ice Giants, she saw a narrow rushing river below, and a woman sitting on an ice ledge on the other side. Lying in the woman's lap was a small medicine bundle decorated with a black raven.

The woman was looking up, watching Twig.

When Twig soared across the river and flew down to get a better look at her, the woman said, "So. You made it across the river into the Land of the Dead. I knew you would. You are strong."

Twig alighted on the ledge a short distance away. The woman was beautiful. Tall and willowy, long black hair framed her oval face. She had full lips and a turned-up nose with coal-black eyes.

"Are you Cobia?"

"I am, child." She wore a white mammoth-hide cape, and a huge bear claw pendant hung in the middle of her chest.

"Please, help us! We need your help to defeat the Thornback raiders. They're killing us!"

Cobia cocked her head. "You have braved great dangers, and therefore earned the right to talk. But I warn you, I'm not going back with you. *You* are their dreamer now."

"Please, Cobia! You have to. We need you!" Twig cried as she balanced on the ledge, thinking about Screech Owl and her mother...and about Greyhawk, who was bravely protecting her even now. They would die if Cobia didn't help them.

Sadness came over Cobia's beautiful face. She patted the ledge beside her. "Come here, child. Let me look at you. You're very young. Too young to have made this difficult journey to the Land of the Dead."

Twig spread her wings, lifted into the air, and softly landed less than four hands from Cobia.

"Yes," Cobia said. "I spend a great deal of time here, talking with my ancestors. Is Screech Owl your teacher?"

"Yes."

Love shone in Cobia's black eyes. She looked away and blinked. "Is he well?"

Tears choked Twig. "He and Mother were captured by the Thornback raiders after they destroyed Buffalobeard Village. Screech Owl may... may be dead."

Cobia slowly lifted her head. "When did this happen?"

Twig tried to think. "I'm not sure. I don't know how long I've been hunting for you. Time—"

"Yes, I know, time is different when you're on a Spirit journey. You may have been gone for moments, or moons. This could be the past, or the future. There's no way to know until you return to your world."

"We need you, Cobia. Screech Owl says you're the only person who can defeat the Thornback raiders. You have to help us."

Cobia gently stroked Twig's speckled brown feathers and whispered, "Did your Grandfather ever tell you why I hate him so?"

Twig blinked. "No."

Cobia smiled faintly. "He is the one who kept the truth from me. For many summers, I spoke to every trader who came from the far west to Buffalobeard Village. I asked each one about the stories my people, the People of the Duskland, told about me. I was a magical child. Everyone knew my name. When your grandfather killed my mother and pulled me from her dead arms, my people saw it as a terrible sign. They believed they had been cursed by the gods. They tracked your grandfather and almost burned him to death in a cave where he ran to hide. But he escaped." Anger lined her face. "I learned the final details of the story just after I'd seen nineteen summers. That's when I left Buffalobeard Village. I vowed never to return, or to help the people who had killed my mother. Do you now understand why I will not go back with you? I knew you needed to grow wings—that's why I kept calling to you in your dreams. But you must save your people by yourself."

Twig was sobbing when she said, "You shouldn't blame us! You could have gone home after you found out what my people did to your mother. Why didn't you?"

Cobia drew her hand back and closed it to a fist.

"Because too much hope can kill as swiftly as a spear, young dreamer. I knew nothing about the People of the Duskland. They were my people by birth, but they were not the people I loved when I was growing up. They were strangers."

"So you decided it was better to be lonely for the rest of your life than to face your fears?"

Cobia's expression softened. She gave Twig a sad smile and petted her feathers again. "You surprise me."

"Why?"

"For just a moment, you became Truth."

"I don't understand."

Cobia frowned out at the icy wilderness that spread before them. "Truth is not in words, young dreamer, but in a reflection, an iridescence that causes us to suddenly turn and look. That's what you just did to me. You made me turn and look. At myself."

Twig cocked her head. "What did you see?"

"Darkness."

In the cavern far below, masks flashed, and ghostly dancers whirled in time to music Twig could not hear. She watched them for a time before she said, "Cobia, please, help us. I know you hate my grandfather, but I didn't do those things to you, nor did my mother. And Screech Owl only tried to help you. He loves you. Won't you at least save him?"

Cobia hesitated. After what seemed an eternity, she stroked Twig's feathered head and said, "The Spirits never give us all the time we need. Your time here is over. You must return now. Greyhawk needs you. *Go back...before it's too late.*"

Twig bowed her head and wept. She had failed. After all the lessons she had learned, all the terrible trials she had faced, Cobia was not going to help her. Sobs clutched at her chest. It was so cold that her tears froze as they fell and tinkled like bells when they struck the ice. She whispered, "I'm sorry. I'm going."

She fluttered her wings and rose above the ice, where she hovered, looking down at the vast icy wilderness below. Then she soared south...

# twenty-four

A bizarre flash of blue light filled the tunnel where Greyhawk sat. He spun around breathlessly, trying to see where it had come from, but the ice cave had turned orange again.

"Once we've eaten," a raider outside said, "we'll pile the last coals from our fires in the tunnel. It won't take long to finish melting out that stubborn patch of ice. Then we'll go in after the brats."

Greyhawk forced a swallow down his throat. The night was very dark, and the raiders' fire cast odd flickering shadows over the tunnel. The wonderful scent of roasted venison kept blowing in, making Greyhawk's empty stomach growl.

A man leaned down and peered into the tunnel. "I want to be the one to go in," he said, and it sounded like Netsink, the man who had attacked him in Buffalobeard Village. "I can't wait to get my hands around the boy's throat."

Greyhawk shivered. No matter what, he wasn't going to leave Twig. When the raider started in, Greyhawk would drag Twig as far as he could. After that, maybe he could fight his way out, then lead the raiders away from the cave long enough for Twig to escape.

The warriors would probably hunt him down, but...

Twig let out a breath, and Greyhawk jumped.

Softly, he called, "Twig? Can you hear me? It's Greyhawk."

Cruel laughter rose outside.

Raiders started carrying bowls of coals and dumping them in the tunnel less than ten hands from where Greyhawk sat. The red glow cast a lurid halo over the ice walls.

"Oh, Twig, please wake up."

Water dripped from the ceiling as the cave continued to melt. The raiders cheered and poured more coals on top of the pile.

Greyhawk got on his knees and slipped his hands beneath Twig's shoulders, preparing to drag her deeper into the tunnel.

# twenty-five

Twig woke with a start when she felt herself being dragged over the icy floor. "Greyhawk?"

"Twig! Oh, thank the Spirits, you're awake!" Greyhawk gently lowered her to the floor again and crouched at her side. "I thought you were dying."

Twig sat up. She had a terrible headache that made her sick to her stomach, but she said, "I did die."

"You did?"

"Yes. I went on a Spirit journey, and my Spirit Helper, Eagle-Man, tore me apart with his beak and swallowed me."

Greyhawk looked at her with wide eyes. "I definitely don't want him for my Spirit Helper."

Twig smiled. "He had to do it. When he pecked away my head, I grew bird eyes, and then I could see the hole in the roof that led to Cobia. I flew across the river and into the Land of the Dead."

"Did you find Cobia?" Greyhawk whispered.

Twig heaved a tired sigh. "Yes."

"Is she coming to help us?"

When tears caught at the back of Twig's throat, her head hurt so badly she thought she'd pass out. She took a deep breath and let it out slowly to calm down. "No, I don't think so."

Greyhawk glanced back down the tunnel at the pile of glowing coals that were melting out the ice. Men had started shoving the pile deeper into the tunnel.

He asked, "Are you well enough to crawl farther back into the tunnel? They'll be coming soon."

"I—I'll try." Twig got on her knees and started crawling.

But it didn't take long.

The tunnel ended in less than fifty heartbeats. Just ended. There was no way out.

Twig leaned against the solid ice wall, breathing hard, her head aching, and Greyhawk positioned himself in front of her, holding Puffer's atlatl like a club...waiting for the raiders.

# twenty-six

In less than two hands of time, the raiders had done it. Twig shivered when they started raking out the piles of glowing coals, clearing a path big enough for a man to slide into the cave.

Greyhawk breathed, "Here they come, Twig," and gripped his atlatl.

The raider who started in was small across the shoulders. His eyes glinted in the red light cast by the few coals that still lined the tunnel. When Twig and Greyhawk slid as far back as they could, pressing hard against the ice wall, the man laughed, "You brats look like cornered chipmunks!"

The man reached for Greyhawk's leg, and Greyhawk bashed his hand with his atlatl. The raider yipped in pain and instead grabbed hold of Twig's foot.

"Greyhawk! He's got me!" Twig shouted.

Greyhawk battered the man's head with his atlatl.

The raider shouted, "Boy, I am going to roast you like a rabbit when we get outside!"

"Try it!" Greyhawk shouted back and kept beating the man in the head and arms.

Twig squirmed and kicked as the raider dragged her down the tunnel and out into the starlight, where he shoved her into the arms of another warrior and said, "Here, Hook. She's all yours."

When Hook clamped his big hand around her arm, Twig shrieked, "Let me go!" and as she struggled to wrench free, her eyes landed on the knife tucked into his belt. The long blade was shining black obsidian. Could she—

Hook ordered, "Go back in and get the boy, Catfish."

The first raider slithered into the tunnel again and, a little while later, dragged Greyhawk out and shoved him hard to the ground.

Greyhawk cried out when Catfish grabbed his atlatl, broke it over his knee, and cast the broken halves out into the darkness, saying, "Now stand up, boy! Just so I can knock you down again!"

Greyhawk, shaking badly, got his feet under him and stood up.

Catfish drew back his hand to knock him down...but Netsink grabbed Greyhawk and dragged him out of the way. "This one is mine."

"No, he's not!" Catfish objected. "Look at my head. He beat me bloody! He should be mine to kill."

"You didn't have to fight off the huge dog he sicced on you! He's mine." Netsink wrenched Greyhawk's arm and flung him to the ground, then he kicked Greyhawk hard in the back and kept kicking him.

Greyhawk grunted, groaned, and rolled into a ball, trying to shield his head from the brutal attack.

When Netsink stopped kicking Greyhawk and pulled a spear from his quiver, hot blood surged through Twig's veins. She dove for Hook's knife.

The war chief had been smiling, watching Netsink. Twig's desperate move took him completely by surprise. He gasped when she ripped the knife from his belt and, before he could stop her, plunged it into his belly.

"*What?*" Hook shouted. He grabbed her wrist and twisted until she cried out and let go of the knife. "The brat stabbed me!"

He slapped Twig hard, and she staggered backward, watching as he jerked the knife from his belly. Dark, foul-smelling blood gushed from the wound.

Twig stared at it and felt sick. What had she done? She'd had no choice, but...her stomach heaved. She rolled to her hands and knees and vomited on the ground, over and over, until there was nothing left to come up. Her head was swimming when she looked back at him.

Hook staggered, dazed. He dipped his hand in the blood and laughed.

The other warriors hissed amongst themselves. The tall raider named Shrike sniffed the air and said, "The girl lanced your guts, Hook. You're as good as dead."

Hook blinked and looked around. "Don't even think—"

Shrike called to the other warriors, "I have been Hook's deputy for three summers. He's dying. You all know this kind of wound. He'll be useless before morning. I now claim the title of war chief."

The hissing grew louder. Some of the raiders smiled their support. Others scowled angrily.

Copper Falcon said, "You are not fit to be our war chief! I challenge you for the right." He stepped forward, drew his knife, and spread his legs, prepared to fight.

Shrike chuckled and drew his knife. The two men began circling each other, jabbing and feinting.

Twig quietly backed away, all the while searching for a place to hide. For the briefest of instants, Greyhawk looked up, and their gazes locked. *Sealing a bargain...*

Neither of them would leave this canyon without the other.

Copper Falcon slashed open Shrike's left arm. At the sight of his blood, the raiders roared.

Hook shouted, "Stop it. We shouldn't be fighting each other! We...we have to..." As though the gut juices were soaking into his veins, poisoning him, he couldn't seem to remember what he'd wanted to say. Then he shouted, "We have to find the Stone Wolf!"

No one paid him any attention. Every eye was on the fight.

Shrike glared at Copper Falcon. "I'm going to

slice your liver out a piece at a time and eat it before your eyes!"

"You arrogant fool!"

Copper Falcon lunged again, but this time, Shrike spun out of the way and landed an elbow in the back of Copper Falcon's neck, staggering him. In the half-a-heartbeat it took Copper Falcon to catch his balance, Shrike plunged his knife into Copper Falcon's kidney and ripped upward.

Copper Falcon shrieked, dropped his knife, and awkwardly pulled his war club from his belt. As he spun around, trying to clip Shrike with a hasty swipe of his club, Shrike kicked the club from Copper Falcon's hand and sent it cartwheeling high into the air.

The raiders cheered and closed in around the two men, waiting for the kill.

Twig looked at Greyhawk, but his eyes were not on her. He was watching the club fall. It landed in the snow three paces from him.

A high-pitched, blood-curdling cry of pain rang out.

Twig jerked around and saw Shrike kick Copper Falcon's feet out from under him. Copper Falcon toppled to the ground, and Shrike was instantly on top of him, plunging his knife into Copper Falcon's chest. Copper Falcon's hideous cries echoed down the canyon.

When the cries stopped, Shrike stumbled to his feet and lifted both arms into the air, shouting, "I am the new war chief!"

Most of the men began dancing, clapping, and

cheering. But two warriors stood to the side, glowering hatefully at Shrike.

Twig silently took a step toward Greyhawk.

And Shrike saw her.

His eyes blazed. "You. Girl. Come over here."

Twig stood rooted to the spot.

Shrike stalked over and grabbed her by the hair. He wrenched her neck around so he could stare down into her eyes and said, "You are Twig, aren't you?"

She refused to answer.

"A boy in your village said you had the Stone Wolf. Where is it?"

Twig tried to stall, to think of something...

"*Where is it?*" He leaned down and shouted the words right in her face.

Twig was shaking so badly her voice seemed to have left her.

Shrike lowered his face until their noses almost touched and hissed, "Tell me now, or you die."

He lifted his bloody knife and placed it against her throat. The sharp edge burned, already cutting into her skin.

"Stop it!" Greyhawk shouted. He got his feet under him and stood up. He was hiding something in his right hand, tucked up into his sleeve.

Shrike laughed. "You little idiot. Catfish, club the boy."

Twig screamed and threw herself sideways, struggling to break free from Shrike's grip...and the Stone Wolf flopped out of her coat and lay shining and black on her chest.

Shrike said, "There it is! I knew you had it."

He grabbed the Wolf and ripped it from Twig's neck. Then he laughed as he looked down at it. "I will be cheered as a hero when I give this to Chief Nightcrow!"

Catfish removed his war club from his belt and stalked toward Greyhawk. When he swung, Greyhawk madly dove out of the way, rolled, and came up with Copper Falcon's war club in his hand. He slammed it into Catfish's lower leg.

Catfish shrieked and dropped to the ground, staring in horror at the broken bone that thrust out of his leg just above his ankle. "The boy broke my leg! *Kill him!*"

Netsink charged after Greyhawk—who was desperately trying to crawl away—kicked the war club from his hand, and grabbed him by the back of the coat. "You're dead, boy."

Twig screamed, *"No!"*

As though she'd triggered it, a fiery gleam swelled on the northern horizon.

Netsink, holding tight to Greyhawk's coat, stammered, "Wh-what's that? Do you see that?" He released Greyhawk to look.

The gleam expanded, growing larger and larger until it filled the entire sky, and they stood in an ocean of orange light. The towering ice walls glittered with it.

"The sky is on fire!" Shrike said and shoved Twig to the ground to squint upward. "Look!"

Far in the north, a rumble started, growing louder, coming toward them...then the gleam exploded! Thousands of Meteor People blasted across the sky, leaving fiery trails, and a rolling wave of flames consumed the heavens.

Greyhawk shouted, "Twig, is this your dream?"

Before she could answer, a thunderous boom split the air, and the concussion knocked all of them off their feet. The boom was followed by a deafening ripping sound, like the sky was being torn apart by the hands of the gods.

The raiders screamed and covered their ears.

Netsink shouted, "What's happening?" but Twig barely heard him.

The ripping sound turned into an inhuman shriek and quickly rose to a constant stunning roar, as though a thousand mountain lions were fighting inside the light.

"Blessed Spirits!" Shrike cried. "The girl is a witch! She's called the Star People down upon us!"

While he was staring upward, Twig scrambled over and jerked the Stone Wolf out of his hand. He didn't even try to take it back. He just kept his terrified eyes on the burning sky.

Twig slipped the Stone Wolf over her head and... saw something move in the black maw of the ice cave.

Twig blinked. "What's that? Greyhawk? Do you see that?"

He whirled around, ready for a fight. "What? Where?"

Twig lifted her arm to point.

Against the charcoal background, a slender woman moved, rushing toward them. Tall and willowy, she wore pure white hides and had long shimmering white hair. She was beautiful, with large dark eyes, full lips, and a turned-up nose. A small medicine bundle decorated with a black raven hung from her belt.

In awe, Twig whispered, "Cobia. It—it's her!"

Greyhawk hissed, "Are you sure?"

In her dream, Cobia had had black hair, but the medicine bundle was the same. "Yes!"

The woman moved quickly, but with such grace, she seemed to be floating through the brilliant orange glare that filled Hoarfrost Canyon. Her black eyes had fixed on Twig. She ran straight for her without saying a word.

The hair at the back of Twig's neck prickled as if stroked by an unseen hand. "Cobia?"

All of the raiders turned to look when they heard her name. A din of shocked cries rose. "It is her! It's really Cobia!"

Thousands of Star People streaked across the sky, leaving brilliant flaming trails as they headed south. And from somewhere in the distance, Twig heard a staccato of thumps as they struck the earth.

Shrike cried, "The Star People are hunting us down! Run and hide! We have to get away!"

He dove for the cave they had melted out to get to Greyhawk and Twig, quickly disappearing inside, as though hiding would protect him from the gods. Another warrior scrambled in after him.

Fluid as a ghost, her white cape swaying around her white moccasins, Cobia grabbed Greyhawk's hand as she passed, dragged him to his feet, and hurried for Twig. "Take my hand!"

Twig gazed into those huge haunted eyes and, for the first time in her life, knew true terror. Power, like a writhing living thing, filled those black depths. She choked out, "Where are you taking us?"

*"Come with me! Now."*

Twig grabbed her hand, and Cobia dragged both children back into her cave just as the earthquake struck like the enormous fist of the Creator.

The impact tossed Twig high into the air and then slammed her face-down on the rocky floor of the cave. The air went out of her lungs, and stunning pain flashed through her entire body. When she looked up, she saw Cobia and Greyhawk lying a short distance away.

Cobia immediately rolled to her side and got on her hands and knees. *"Follow me! We must get deeper into my cave!"* She started crawling.

Greyhawk was right behind her, but after five heartbeats, he turned back to look for Twig. "Twig? Come on!"

She still couldn't breathe, couldn't seem to make her lungs suck in air. She tried to call to him for help, but no sound came up her throat. Her mouth moved in pitiful cries that no one could hear, not even Cobia.

Outside, the Thornback raiders screamed. Twig jerked to look and saw a huge green ball of light tumble across the sky right over their heads, followed by what sounded like millions of lightning bolts crackling through the air at once. For long moments, the raiders just stared up. Time might have stopped.

Then, there was a blinding flash...and a searing wave of heat struck.

Without thinking, Twig threw up her arms to cover her face, but her skin seemed to catch fire! It was like being thrown into raging flames!

An instant later, hurricane-force wind blasted the world. It picked her up like a feather and hurled her back into the cave, where it bashed her into solid rock and kept her pinned there. After one hundred heartbeats, the wind stopped. Just stopped.

Twig fell to the floor, gasping for breath, and saw the huge blisters that covered her arms. Her face must look the same way.

She tried to get to her feet, but the Ice Giants let out a magnificent, terrifying roar, and the earthquake smashed her down again. The land itself seemed to be splitting wide open, shattering into splinters of rock and ice that no one could ever piece together again.

Fog rolled into the cave, thick, as though the Ice Giants were vaporizing outside.

Twig tried to shout at Greyhawk and could tell he was shouting back. His mouth was moving, but his voice was drowned out by the earthquake.

Greyhawk and Twig madly slid forward on their bellies until they could clasp hands.

Ahead, deeper in the cave, Cobia was waving them forward and shouting, though they couldn't hear her.

Together, they scrambled across the heaving

floor to get to her...and she led them back, deeper and deeper into the darkness.

When Twig dared to glance back through the mouth of the cave, she saw the fog burning red and glowing gravel raining down...and water. Water was filling Hoarfrost Canyon.

The Ice Giants were flooding the world.

# twenty-seven

Howling wind blew clouds of dust and smoke up the trail, and the air had a lurid crimson gleam. Screech Owl pulled Riddle's good arm over his shoulders and supported her as they followed the lake trail behind the rest of the Buffalobeard Village survivors, fifteen in all. Each had been badly burned when the sky exploded two days ago. But they were alive. Everywhere he looked, he saw devastation. The Ice Giants, covered with dust and soot, had turned black as night. Vast clouds of steam rose from them and shrouded Ice Giant Lake with fog.

Right after the explosion, the lake had started rising, and by the next morning, all of the charred remains of Buffalobeard Village were underwater. They had no choice but to leave, to search for another place to start a new village. Screech Owl feared they would have to travel west for a very long time before they escaped the choking haze that filled the world here.

Riddle winced and moaned.

"How are you doing?" Screech Owl asked her. "Do you need to rest?"

"No. We can't afford to fall behind." She'd broken her arm when the roof collapsed on top of her. Now, she wore it in a hide sling. Clearly in pain, she kept uttering soft sounds of anguish. "The dust is so thick, we may get lost. But thank you for asking." She tipped up her blistered, soot-coated face to smile her thanks at him.

He smiled back, and they kept walking.

From somewhere up ahead, he heard Halfmoon call, "Everyone, stay within sight of the person in front of you! Hold your children's hands. We don't want to lose anyone!"

Screech Owl kept his gaze on Reef's muscular back. The tall warrior had his atlatl in his hand, as always, and a quiver of spears slung over his shoulder. He kept turning around to look back, making sure everyone was still in sight. Many of the old people and children were stumbling, having trouble breathing, and many more were wounded. Now and then, Screech Owl caught sight of a bloody bandage encircling an arm or leg. A constant noise of coughing, wheezing, and crying children filled the air.

Oddly, the pack of dogs that trailed in the rear were silent as ghosts.

The orphaned children walked in a single group near the front. Through the blowing dust, he saw

Grizzly towering over the others. The boy had his thumb in his mouth, sucking it for comfort. Poor child. He had lost both his mother and father. At least his brother Little Cougar was standing beside him, holding Grizzly's sleeve in a tight grip. Rattler carried a baby girl in her arms. Screech Owl had no idea who the baby belonged to. But it didn't matter now. They had only one goal, to survive. And to do that, they had to take care of each other.

When they reached the crest, Halfmoon stopped and shielded his eyes to look up the trail. Had Searobin returned? At dawn, Halfmoon had dispatched the warrior to scout the trails ahead.

They were under no illusions. If they were fleeing westward to escape the fiery destruction, so were the Thornback People. As well as every short-faced bear and dire wolf that had lived. And all of them would be hungry.

Riddle asked, "What's Father doing?"

"I'm not sure." Screech Owl thought he saw a dark shape moving farther up the trail. "I think he's waiting. There's someone on the trail ahead."

"Searobin? He's back? Is he safe?"

The man came into view, trotting steadily forward.

"I don't see any wounds, but let's go find out."

He carefully led Riddle down the hill and into the group. Halfmoon spoke briefly with Searobin before he turned, looked around with his white-filmed eyes, and said, "Reef? Is everyone here?"

"Yes, Elder. All fifteen of us. We're still together."

People stood with scraps of hide pressed over their noses to block the dust and smoke, and their eyes squinted against the icy wind. Tears had mixed with the debris to form muddy trails down their faces.

Halfmoon held up a hand and called, "I know you are all exhausted and hungry, but we have to keep moving. Searobin just brought news that it's much worse to the south. There are fires everywhere. The forests are all blazing. That's where the smoke is coming from."

Searobin coughed and cleared his throat before calling, "We are lucky to be at the edge of the lake! You can breathe here because of the fog. It keeps most of the smoke away. Farther south, I saw dead animals and people lying everywhere. It looks like they suffocated where they were standing when the star exploded."

People shifted and stared. No one knew what to say. It sounded like the end of the world.

Halfmoon said, "So we must keep moving west. Now! Let's go."

He turned to start up the trail again, and Riddle called, "Father? Father, please wait. What about Twig and Greyhawk? They are out there somewhere. Alone. Shouldn't we wait for them?"

Halfmoon's mouth tightened. He must be as worried about Twig as Riddle was, but as a warrior, he probably assumed his granddaughter was dead. He squared his shoulders and called, "We can't. It's too dangerous. We don't know where the Thornback People are. The safety of everyone is at risk.

We must keep moving. But..." He coughed and looked around at the scared villagers. "You should all know that my granddaughter dreamed this. She told me about the exploding star a quarter moon ago. I—"

"Yes," old Bandtail agreed. "Halfmoon told us of her dreams, but we didn't believe him. Twig was so young—"

"Is so young," Screech Owl corrected. "Twig may be the greatest dreamer our people have ever known. She's alive. I know it. The Spirits of our ancestors would not have let her die."

Bandtail exhaled hard. The old woman's blackened face looked strangely purple. "If only we had listened to her dream, by now, we would be far to the west, away from this destruction."

Murmuring broke out, and people began nodding their heads.

Riddle bowed her head and nodded, too—but Screech Owl saw the tears that cut lines through the mud on her cheeks. She whispered, "I should have told the elders about her dreams long ago. We would be even farther to the west. And Twig would be with us."

Screech Owl said, "She will find us, Riddle."

Riddle gave him a brave smile, but she clearly didn't believe him. How could she? Wind blasted the trail, scouring it clean every instant. There would be no tracks to follow.

Halfmoon led them down the trail into a dense choking cloud of red-hued dust.

Screech Owl repositioned Riddle's arm over his shoulders and whispered, "Twig will dream her way to us. You'll see."

"Do you think so? Truly?" Her voice trembled.

"I *know* so."

# twenty-eight

The fog bled pink, then burned orange, and finally became a shimmering scarlet blanket. As Twig marched through it behind Cobia and Greyhawk, she no longer felt human. She pressed the hide over her nose and fought to breathe. Her senses had sharpened like those of a threatened animal. She could hear, smell, and taste the danger that ghosted by on the howling wind. The ground almost never stopped shaking, and the deep-throated groans and shrieks of the dying Ice Giants were constant.

Over the past three days, she had seen things she never wanted to see again: charred headless corpses, blown into a tangled heap by the hurricane, and herds of animals moving with their noses to the ground, trying to sniff out trails because their eyes had been roasted in their heads.

Twig and Greyhawk picked up weapons every chance they got. Both of them carried atlatls in their hands and quivers of spears over their shoulders. They had stone knives tied to their belts.

Only Cobia had no weapons. Perhaps because she didn't need any.

Twig lifted her nose and smelled the air. It was heavy with the scents of burning hickory and spruce and a strange sulfur-like smell that reminded her of rotten eggs.

All day long, she had thought about Bison Calf, wondering if this was how he had felt on the last day of his life. She remembered the desperate sound of his cries, as though he'd been calling for his mother or his herd, praying someone would come and save him from the human hunters. Bison Calf could not have known he was the last of his kind in the world. He must have been terrified.

As Twig was.

Twig closed her eyes and prayed that Bison Calf's soul had found its way to the Land of the Dead and that he would never be frightened again, or hungry, or lonely.

Greyhawk shouted, "Who is that?" and Twig jerked her eyes open.

A human figure appeared to Twig's left, startling her. She grabbed for her knife.

It was an old man. He stepped out of the dense fog, and Cobia stopped to speak with him. Twig could hear their voices but not the words. The man clutched his elk-hide hood tightly beneath his chin.

Cobia shouted something in his ear, and the old man shook his head and shouted back, *"All dead...the end of the world...nowhere to hide."*

Had she asked him about his family, or his village?

Cobia said something else, and it seemed as though she was trying to talk him into going with them, but he shook his head again and drifted back into the fog, disappearing as though he'd never been.

Greyhawk turned around and, through the hide held over his nose, said, "Did you hear that?"

"No. What did he say?"

"He said that evil Spirits rode in with the bursting star and were roaming the world, killing every human still alive. His entire village was slaughtered."

Sensibly, she answered, "His evil Spirits are probably Thornback warriors."

"Yes, probably."

Greyhawk turned back when Cobia continued down the trail, and they walked in single file for another four hands of time without saying a word to each other.

Just before nightfall, when the temperature began to plummet, they came to a river. A black river. Dead fish floated on the surface. So much soot and ash had mixed with the water it ran like liquid coal. If Twig lived long enough to have children, would they ever believe her?

"Are we stopping?" Greyhawk called to Cobia.

She turned around with her long white hair—turned gray with ash—whipping around her face and shouted, "No! We keep going until we are ready to drop in our tracks. We must get away from this devastation." She waded the river. It came up to her knees, and to Greyhawk's hips.

When Twig stepped in, she gasped at the cold. The water was absolutely freezing, as though it had just poured from the mouths of the Ice Giants. On the other side, she stood shivering. She had totally lost her bearings, with no idea whether they were headed north, south, east, or west.

She said, "Greyhawk, what direction are we headed? South?"

"West," he corrected. "Due west."

"How do you know? There's too much fog and smoke to see the sun."

He shrugged. "I just know. We're headed west."

In another twenty paces, the fog suddenly parted, and Twig blinked. Ten paces away, there was a mammoth perched on a boulder. Cobia and Greyhawk saw it, too. They both pointed.

Mammoth's shaggy hair had been burned off, leaving red blistered hide behind. It was seated on its haunches, staring out at the dust storm, as though totally lost and trying to find some familiar landmark to lead it back to its herd. When Mammoth spotted Twig, they studied each other, then the mammoth again looked at the dust and lifted its trunk to trumpet into the storm. It cocked its head, waited to hear an answer, and trumpeted again.

The only sound Twig heard was the shrill howling of the wind.

But Mammoth seemed to hear something else. It stood up, listened, and clambered awkwardly off the boulder. It started walking out across the vast wasteland.

Cobia's eyes narrowed. She watched the mammoth as though their very lives depended upon it.

Then she turned. "Do either of you have Mammoth as a Spirit Helper?"

Greyhawk said, "Not me."

Twig shook her head.

Cobia hesitated a few heartbeats longer before stepping into the tracks of the mammoth and following. In the eerie, gaudy light, the animal seemed magical. Its big body faded in and out of the fog, and often, it seemed to be waiting for them to catch up. They would lose sight of the mammoth, then find it standing still in the wavering mist, looking back. When they caught up, it started walking again.

As they wandered through the smoke and fog, they coughed until their lungs ached. Their bellies gnawed at their backbones from hunger, but they kept going.

# twenty-nine

Four days later, the smoke cleared a little. They could see farther. Mammoth continued to lead the way, but now she was one hundred paces ahead and still in sight, whereas the day before, if Mammoth was twenty paces ahead, they couldn't see her.

The strange new sounds haunted Twig. There were no birds chirping or caribou calling. No sounds of life. Night was the worst. The wind became a growling monster, and it was achingly cold. They had no hides and no time to make a fire. When they rested, they curled into shallow pits to sleep for a few heartbeats or took shelter behind boulders. But never for long. They all knew they might never wake up.

Mammoth suddenly looked back at them.

Cobia stopped. Greyhawk and Twig ran to see what she was looking at.

Greyhawk said, "It...it's Tidewater Village. Isn't it?"

Long ago, when Twig had seen eight summers, Mother had brought her here to visit Uncle Banded Bear. Just as she remembered, the caves of Tidewater Village overlooked Ice Giant Lake, but four summers ago, the glistening blue lake had been far in the distance. Today, its filthy black water washed into the caves, swallowing them. Ominously, several caves had been rocked up, as though the villagers had tried to hold back the flood. From the corpses, she knew they'd failed.

"Yes," Cobia softly answered. "It *was* Tidewater Village."

Her eyes scanned the bodies. Some hung out of the caves; others floated in the distance like tiny islands.

Twig felt as though she'd staggered into the middle of a battlefield. Everywhere, everyone was dead. She sniffed the air and smelled their rot.

"Why didn't they leave their caves and run?" Greyhawk asked Cobia.

She shook her head slightly. "Whatever they saw outside must have been more frightening than the possibility of drowning."

Greyhawk gripped his atlatl and looked around.

They all did, searching for that threat.

But only the bloody mist and scorched land answered.

Mammoth started walking again.

They followed.

# thirty

After another day, they found a shore where icebergs had been blown by the ferocious winds and grounded. Ten times the height of a man, they had lined up on the sand and resembled an enormous jaw filled with broken, black teeth.

Cobia said, "Let's sit down and rest out of the wind for a few moments."

Twig and Greyhawk slumped to the ground and heaved heavy sighs.

Cobia used a rock to chip away the filthy surface of an iceberg and handed them each a chunk of ice to suck on. While Twig and Greyhawk rested, Cobia walked down the shore, picking up dead fish. The entire shoreline was coated with them. Cobia tossed many away—too rotten, probably—and came back with six fish. She handed two to Greyhawk and two to Twig. Twig studied her fish. The slimy skin was falling off the meat. They stank.

"Don't think," Cobia said. "Just eat."

Twig pulled off the rotting skin and closed her eyes. She ate without breathing, so she couldn't smell them. And her empty stomach was grateful. When they started walking again, she felt stronger.

They walked all night, following the mammoth, shivering.

By morning, she knew something had changed. The gaudy red glow that had announced dawn for the past six days was gone. Instead, Father Sun rose somewhere beyond the dense clouds of smoke and ash and cast a surreal grayish-yellow light on the world.

As the light brightened, they saw Mammoth, and beyond her, dark shapes on the trail.

"Cobia?" Twig called. "Are those people?"

Greyhawk reached for a spear and nocked his atlatl in case they were Thornback warriors. "Where, Twig? I don't see them."

"There. In front of Mammoth."

Shouts rose from up ahead. The people had seen them...or perhaps they were hungry and had seen Mammoth.

Twig's belly muscles went tight with fear.

Mammoth lifted her trunk and trumpeted as though signaling victory...and then she charged off at full speed, heading south into the denser smoke.

Ahead, people gathered on the trail, staring back at Twig, and she thought...but she was afraid to hope...

"Who are they?" Greyhawk asked. He had his spear up, ready to cast.

Cobia said, "I think they are People of the Dawnland. See the way they dress?"

Greyhawk's eyes widened. He lowered his spear. "Are you sure?"

Twig's heart suddenly ached so desperately for her mother that she couldn't stand it any longer. She broke into a trot, swerved around Cobia, and dashed headlong up the rocky ridge that curved around the lake.

She could hear Greyhawks steps right behind her. As she raced forward, he called, "Twig! Wait! They could be enemy warriors!"

Breathing hard, her heart about to burst, she ran harder.

The people watched her, and...

*"Twig!"* Mother cried and shoved through the crowd. She had her arm in a sling, and her face was coated with soot and grime. "Twig? Look! Screech Owl, *it's Twig and Greyhawk!"*

Mother started running back for them, and everyone else in the village followed her. Screech Owl lifted a hand to Twig, and she waved back.

Greyhawk's father, Reef, shouted, "Greyhawk!"

Yipper, who had been standing at Reef's side, wildly spun around to look. The dog's head had a bandage wrapped tightly all the way around it.

When Yipper saw Greyhawk, he took off running like a spear cast from an atlatl, bounding up the trail as though desperate to make certain Greyhawk was safe.

Greyhawk knelt in the trail and opened his arms. "Yipper! Yipper, come here, boy!"

The dog launched himself into Greyhawk's arms, knocked him flat, and started ferociously licking his face while Greyhawk squirmed and laughed.

Mother hurried up the trail and fell to her knees to hug Twig. Crying, she said, "Oh, Twig, I was so afraid! I love you. I love you."

When Cobia crested the ridge, Mother suddenly released Twig, staggered to her feet, and whispered, *"Cobia."*

Cobia stared at Mother through bottomless, pitch-black eyes and said, "Yes, I'm back."

Cobia walked over the crest and down the trail... and as people began to recognize her, the world seemed to stop. No one moved. No one spoke. Not even the dogs barked at her. No one had seen her in twenty summers—not since she'd killed Chief Minnow with a breath across her palm.

Then her whispered name began to pass through the villagers like the hiss of a serpent: *"Cobia. It's Cobia."*

Screech Owl suddenly broke away from the crowd.

He ran up the trail and embraced Cobia in a powerful hug. "I'm so glad you're safe. Thank you for bringing Twig and Greyhawk home."

Cobia said, "I didn't. Mammoth led us here."

"Did she?"

"Yes. I think Twig may have a Spirit Helper she does not yet know."

# thirty-one

Nightcrow felt old. He shivered in the freezing wind as it gusted across the top of the hill. He had led his people away from the worst of the destruction, but the fires were coming. He could see a wall of flames in the distance, racing across the hills as though pushed by hurricane winds. He could also see the two men running toward the makeshift village they had thrown up last night. Both wore black shirts. So, two of his warriors had survived. Others must also see them, for yelling and shouts filtered through the smoky air. People began to run out to meet them. He waited.

In a few hundred heartbeats, Shrike and Black-foot came trotting up the trail to the hilltop. Both smelled of sour sweat and old blood.

Nightcrow blurted, "Tell me quickly. Are you the only survivors?"

Shrike nodded. His face was soot-blackened and

streaked with tears from squinting against the smoke. "Yes, my chief. Everyone else is dead."

Blackfoot wiped his grimy forehead on his sleeve. "The girl is a powerful witch. When Shrike tore the Stone Wolf from her neck, she called down the Star People to kill us."

Nightcrow peered out at the blazing forests, wondering where she was. "The *girl* did this? A little girl?"

"Yes, and she killed Hook, knifed him in the belly."

Shrike nodded. "Even worse, Cobia is her ally." He dropped his voice to a whisper when he said her name, and fear lit his eyes. "Just before the searing heat struck, Cobia ran from her cave and dragged the children inside to protect them."

Nightcrow studied his frightened expression. He held out a hand. "Give me the Stone Wolf."

Shrike shifted his weight to his other foot. "When the Star People started shooting down at us, I—I lost it. I—"

Blackfoot's gaze flicked at Shrike; then quickly, he looked away. Nightcrow clenched his fists in understanding and asked, "Now, tell me the truth. What happened to the Stone Wolf?"

Shrike seemed surprised. He just stared at Nightcrow.

"Go on. Tell him," Blackfoot said.

When Shrike kept his mouth closed, Blackfoot said, "The girl grabbed it from his hand and ran away with it."

In an unsettlingly soft voice, Nightcrow asked,

"And how did you two survive, while the others did not?"

"We dove into an ice cave and hid until the rising water drove us out; then we swam away."

As silent as Eagle's shadow, Nightcrow rose to his feet to face Shrike. "You were Hook's deputy. You abandoned your men?"

"It's not my fault! The others," Shrike gestured as though it was of little concern, "could have scrambled into a cave. They did not."

Nightcrow smiled, and Shrike smiled back, not realizing the source of his chief's amusement. "I see." He pulled out the sacred stiletto, the one Hook had stolen from Starhorse Village, from his belt.

"No, you do not see! There were dark Spirits all around us. The only thing that saved us was that we kept repeating your name. Over and over! We screamed your name! It must have scared Cobia because neither she nor the girl came after us. You are the only reason we made it back alive. Your power shielded us!"

Nightcrow hesitated, his stiletto perfectly still, the carved bone shining red in the strange light. There was something in the way Shrike's devious eyes burned. It was like gazing at a trapped wolf. Nightcrow studied him. He was clearly waiting for the stroke that would end his life.

"Is that true, Blackfoot? Is that how it happened? My name shielded you?"

"Yes, my chief," Blackfoot answered, but his face showed no emotion at all.

Nightcrow smiled again. They might still be useful. He put a hand on Shrike's shoulder and could feel the man trembling. "Well, then, you are brave indeed, Shrike. I name you my new war chief."

Shrike, who had clearly been expecting a blow to the heart, straightened as though he had not heard right. "My chief?"

"Yes, I want you to lead our warriors. You can start by running down this hill and telling everyone your story. Tell them how my name saved you from Cobia's wrath."

"Of course." He glanced at Blackfoot. "We will tell them Cobia *ran* at the sound of your name. We will shout the truth to the—"

"After that," Nightcrow interrupted, "I want you to find the People of the Dawnland and capture the girl."

"Yes, my chief."

As Nightcrow tramped down the hill toward the villagers who were waiting below, he heard Shrike let out a happy whoop.

The fool. He understood nothing.

# thirty-two

By noon, the survivors of the People of the Dawnland marched through an eerily quiet black blizzard. Twig cast a glance over her shoulder. The fires in the south were spreading through the forests, and ash fell like charcoal snowflakes. All of the animals had fled in front of the fires. Not a single deer or buffalo could be seen anywhere. Even the slow-moving sloths had vanished.

Screech Owl and Cobia walked out front. Twig, Greyhawk, and Yipper came next in line, and several more paces back, Mother whispered with Grandfather.

Though many people seemed frightened of Cobia, no one complained about her presence. In fact, they seemed strangely comforted to have the most powerful dreamer in the world leading them.

Twig coughed and tried to breathe. It wasn't easy. The smoke and dust were so thick they were all having trouble breathing. Many people walked with their hide collars held over their noses. But coughs and wheezes filtered down the line.

And in the strange black blizzard, Twig kept seeing things. Huge things, moving around Cobia.

Greyhawk, who was walking beside her, said, "What's wrong, Twig? You keep staring at Cobia."

She turned to him. He had the front of his face tucked down inside his coat so that only his eyes showed. "Do you see them?"

Greyhawk frowned. "See what?"

"I think...nothing. I'm probably just tired. My eyes are playing tricks, but—"

Yipper let out a sudden sharp bark, charged forward, and leaped into the air beside Cobia, snapping at something. Screech Owl and Cobia had their heads together, talking. They didn't even seem to notice him. But Twig and Greyhawk did. When Yipper landed, he stalked around stiff-legged with his hair standing straight up, whining and growling.

Greyhawk's eyes widened. He carefully searched the torrent of black snowflakes before saying to Twig, "Should I be afraid?"

Yipper trotted back toward them, but he kept looking over his shoulder, growling as though in warning.

Twig whispered, "Do you remember the story Elder Bandtail told about Cobia? About the—"

"About the armless things that danced around her bed when she was a child?" Greyhawk hissed. "Is that what you and Yipper see?"

"I think so, but I don't think they're evil. I—"

Two paces ahead, she heard Screech Owl ask Cobia, "The Thornback raiders are behind us, aren't they?"

Cobia's head dipped in a single nod. It had been so subtle people farther back in line would have never seen it, so it could not terrify them the way it did Twig and Greyhawk.

Screech Owl nodded and exhaled hard. "I thank the Spirits that you are here. Have you dreamed where we should go? Where we will be safe?"

Cobia stopped in the trail and waited for Twig and Greyhawk to catch up. When she looked at Twig, her eyes shimmered. "Where will we be safe, Twig? Have you dreamed of it?"

Twig hesitated.

Greyhawk asked, "What's she talking about, Twig?"

Twig took a deep breath, then softly answered, "I—I keep seeing things, and the Stone Wolf is pulling me due west. I think we have to go all the way to the Duskland."

"The Duskland?" Greyhawk half shouted. "Why?"

The other villagers heard him and stopped.

Twig wet her lips, afraid to answer. Cobia had told her that too much hope could kill. Finally, she said, "There is still sunlight there, Greyhawk. Towering trees grow along the coast, and there's plenty of fish and animals. If we can just get there..."

People came forward, surrounding her. The faces of the elders were especially serious. They all listened intently for her next words.

Twig blinked, astonished.

Elder Bandtail hobbled forward. "Are we on the right path to get there, Dreamer?"

"Yes."

Elder Snapper shouldered through the crowd next. "How long will it take us?"

"I don't know, Elder. Many moons, I think." Twig picked up the Stone Wolf, and it tugged her onward, due west.

Everyone seemed to be waiting for her.

Slowly, hesitantly, Twig walked out in front of them, taking the lead.

Cobia, Greyhawk, and Screech Owl fell into line behind her, and the others followed. They followed her—Twig, daughter of Riddle and Screech Owl, a child of the Blue Bear Clan of the People of the Dawnland.

When she looked back over her shoulder, Screech Owl gave her a proud smile.

Twig smiled back, and as she led them down the winding trail toward the far, far Duskland, hope swelled her heart.

She started to walk faster, and Greyhawk called, "Twig, wait for me!"

He ran up to walk beside her, and Yipper shot out in front of them, running down the trail with his tail wagging.

Greyhawk whispered, "I always knew you were a dreamer."

She turned to look at his soot-coated face. "I only made it to Cobia's cave because of you. You are the bravest warrior I will ever know."

Greyhawk smiled, and they both focused on the ash-coated trail ahead.

As she walked, ghostly images formed in the smoke, twisting and shimmering. Somewhere out there, a mammoth trumpeted loudly, tying itself to the forming vision.

Twig stopped suddenly—as the vision became her world.

*I see the smoke break, and ahead of me is Mammoth, looking back over her shoulder, waiting for me to catch up. Her long, silky brown hair has grown back. Her ivory tusks shine, and her eyes are bright and happy. My fear slips away like Buffalo's winter coat in spring. I trot to the crest, my lungs heaving, and suck in an awed breath.*

*Below, thick grasses waver beneath the caress of Wind Woman. Green meadows roll all the way down to touch a vast blue ocean, where wolf pups roll on their backs in the sand, biting their toes before tumbling sideways, then rising and chasing each other along the shore. Their playful yips are like music on the sea-scented breeze. And far out in the grass, Mammoth runs, greeting Caribou, Fox, and Raven as she heads for the herd of mammoths that stand belly-deep in wildflowers. When the other mammoths see her, they trumpet wildly. The entire herd rushes to meet her. They surround her, trumpeting, tossing their heads, and gently smoothing their trunks along her sides and over her back in greeting—as though their lost sister has returned home, and they are joyous.*

*I smile. The air is filled with birdsong and brilliant sunlight.*

*I can barely hear myself whisper, "The Duskland. This is the Duskland..."*

# afterword

Why did the Laurentide Ice Sheet collapse and cause the draining of Lake Agassiz? Scientists have recently discovered that around this same time, a comet may have exploded over the Great Lakes and eastern Canada. Archaeologists have always been fascinated by the strange "black mat" that covers most Clovis culture sites. Clovis archaeological sites date to between 13,500 years ago and 12,900 years ago and are never found above this carbon-rich mat. Clovis culture is best known for the beautiful "fluted" spear points its people made to harvest mammoths, mastodons, and buffalo.

Thanks to the efforts of two physicists, the black mat was recently analyzed and found to contain high amounts of iridium, plus carbon spherules and tiny lumps of glasslike carbon that can best be explained by the explosion of a comet in the earth's atmosphere. When the comet exploded, fragments shot out and slammed into the land, leaving over one million depressions that today we call the Carolina Bays. The impacts set off forest fires and undoubtedly caused the collapse of the Laurentide Ice Sheet that still covered most of Canada east of the Rockies.

If a comet did explode around 12,900 years ago, it must have happened when the comet entered the atmosphere because we have no gaping hole, no crater to mark its point of impact. Scientists speculate that it was an extinction-level event. When the comet struck, it superheated the atmosphere and sent a shock wave across North America, causing one of the largest firestorms in the history of the world. A few seconds after the explosion, a blast of high-pressure wind, over 300 miles per hour, swept the continent; then red-hot debris started falling. About thirty minutes later, a tsunami 600 feet high, consisting of dozens of massive waves, rolled across the oceans, devastating coastlines around the world.

It took years for the clouds of debris, dust, and smoke to finally settle. By then, the world had been thrown back into another Ice Age that we call the Younger Dryas.

But human beings survived, as did buffalo, deer, elk, and most other life-forms.

The journey ahead was difficult, but the adventures of Twig and Greyhawk had only just begun...

# a reader's guide to children of the dawnland part one and two

## ABOUT THIS GUIDE

The information, activities, and discussion questions that follow are intended to enhance your reading of *Children of the Dawnland*. Please feel free to adapt these materials to suit your needs and interests.

## WRITING AND RESEARCH ACTIVITIES
### I. CLOVIS CULTURE

A. Go to the library or online to learn more about Clovis and pre-Clovis archaeological sites across North America. Divide into small groups to create informative posters about individual sites and how discoveries made there have contributed to our understanding of ancient human history.

B. Go to the library or online to learn more about mammoths and other megafauna (great beasts) that became extinct around the end of the Ice Age. On a large (at least 4' X 6') paper surface, create a mural depicting great beasts in their late Ice Age habitat, using information from your research. On index cards, list 4-5 facts about each beast depicted in your mural.

C. Divide into four groups to debate the question: How did the megafauna become extinct? Each group should argue in favor of two of the following theories: (1) overhunting by humans, (2) climate change, (3) disease, (4) an extraterrestrial impact. When the discussion is over, have each group reassess their conclusions to include, if they think it's appropriate, information presented by the other groups. Go to the library or online to research these positions.

## II. DREAMS AND DREAMERS

A. Research and write a short report about the role of dreams in African American, Native American, Chinese, or another culture. Learn to make a Native American dream catcher or study the importance of the mandala in Hinduism and Buddhism. Think of a favorite novelist, musician, or visual artist who explores the theme of dreams and study one of his or her dream-related works.

B. Twig's dreams suggest a troubling fate for her people. Use chalk, watercolor paints, or other visual arts media to depict a scene from one of Twig's dreams. Share your completed artwork with friends or classmates and invite them to share their drawings or paintings. Are colors, images, or other elements common to several pictures? What was most challenging or exciting about trying to depict a dream through art?

C. Review passages in the novel in which Twig experiences powerful dreams. Examine the word choice, point-of-view, tense, sentence structure, and other elements of these passages. Then, in a style inspired by the novel, write your own 2-3 paragraph dream story. It can be based on a real, recalled dream, or a fictional dream idea.

## III. CHANGE

A. With friends or classmates, take turns role-playing a conversation between Twig and Greyhawk in which you discuss the animals you encounter, such as terns and short-faced bears, and those which have disappeared, such as mammoths. How do you feel when elders tell stories of extinct animals? Do you worry about the melting Ice Giants or other natural occurrences? Can you imagine what your world will look like when you are Twig's grandfather's age?

B. Twig and her people live in a time of great climatic change. In addition to a threatened environment, our world is undergoing dramatic economic and environmental changes. Divide a sheet of paper into two columns headed, "Prehistoric Changes" and "Modern Day Changes," listing at least five changes for each below. Compare and contrast the lists. Does this exercise help you better understand Twig's world? How might Twig's story help you gain perspective on what is happening in the world today? Write a 2-3 paragraph essay discussing one or two comparisons which you find particularly interesting.

## DISCUSSION QUESTIONS

1. From whose viewpoint is Chapter One told? What does this perspective help readers learn about the world in which the story takes place? What elements of the landscape seem frightening or worrisome to you?

2. What are the Ice Giants? How are their actions explained and understood by Twig, her mother and their people? What are Thunderbirds and Cloud People? What do such names reveal about the prehistoric peoples' understanding of natural occurrences, such as rain?

3. Who is Cobia? Why was Twig's grandfather sent to kidnap Cobia as a child? Why are warriors from Buffalobeard Village sent to find Cobia? What happens to the warriors?

4. How does Chapter Eight change your understanding of Twig's character and your sense of the story? How does this chapter, and other dream chapters, make the novel unique? Do you believe in Twig's dreams? Explain your answer.

5. What frightens Twig about her Spirit dreaming powers? What makes her nonetheless want to understand her dreams? If you were Twig, would you keep your dreams a secret? Why or why not?

6. In Chapter Eleven, Twig asks Greyhawk and Grizzly "Do you want the buffalo to go away forever, like the mammoths have?" What is important about her question? How does it help readers to better understand the time in which Twig lives? What resources do we fear losing in our own time? What other modern-day comparisons might you make to Twig's concern for the buffalo?

7. Why does Riddle finally allow Twig to study with Screech Owl? What does Screech Owl mean when he tells Twig that ". . . every great Dreamer, at some point, must step into the mouth of the Spirit that wants to chew her up" (Chapter Sixteen)? How might this also be an important piece of wisdom for Twig's entire community? Does it have meaning for modern leaders?

8. How does Water Snake's spirit help Twig elude the Thornback raiders? What terrors does Greyhawk witness? How does Twig persuade Greyhawk to continue their search for Cobia, despite their village being raided?

9. What happens when Twig calls for her spirit helper, Eagle-Man? How does this terrifying moment lead her to Cobia? Is Cobia a real person, a spirit, or another type of being in her early conversation with Twig? Explain your answer.

10. How does Cobia protect Twig and Greyhawk? How do Twig's dreams help lead her back to her people? Where does Twig tell the Sunpath People they must go? How do you understand the relationship between Twig and Cobia at the end of the story?

11. Do you think it is important that the final paragraphs of the novel are told from Twig's dream viewpoint? How does the Afterword affect your understanding of the novel's end? Had you been Twig, would you have had the courage to dream and to embark on a journey to the Duskland? Why or why not? Do you ever feel you need a similar type of courage to face the changes in your own life? Explain your answer.

12. When it comes to climate change, is it possible that this period of global warming is just the beginning of a new Ice Age?

# a look at: skitterbrain
## By Irene Bennett Brown

*From award-winning author Irene Bennett Brown comes a heartwarming story of a young pioneer girl who wanted only one thing out of life and would not give up until she found it.*

When Larnie Moran finds her family's milk cow gone, she knows she's the one at fault. The Morans have to have that cow, for Larnie's sickly mother is about to have a child, and the infant will need milk.

Larnie can not—will not—ask her Papa to get Bessie back for her and risk being called a "skitterbrain" once again. Instead, she follows a large cattle herd across the empty prairie in search of the runaway cow—just in time to see it join a passing trail herd and lose itself among the thousands of steers.

Along the trail to Wichita, she runs into Buzzard, a tough boy younger than she but a lot stronger, who scornfully orders her to go home. Nearly made prisoner by a mad, lonely woman seeking her lost family, befriended by a sodbuster family and discovering that she will have to search through twenty thousand heads of beef steers for her lone cow, her journey is nothing but easy.

*Follow this high-spirited young frontier heroine in a wild and wooly adventure rich in history and female courage.*

**AVAILABLE NOW**

# about w. michael gear

**W. Michael Gear** is a *New York Times, USA Today,* and international bestselling author of sixty novels. With close to eighteen million copies of his books in print worldwide, his work has been translated into twenty-nine languages.

Gear has been inducted into the Western Writers Hall of Fame and the Colorado Authors' Hall of Fame—as well as won the Owen Wister Award, the Golden Spur Award, and the International Book Award for both Science Fiction and Action Suspense Fiction. He is also the recipient of the Frank Waters Award for lifetime contributions to Western writing.

Gear's work, inspired by anthropology and archaeology, is multilayered and has been called compelling, insidiously realistic, and masterful. Currently, he lives in northwestern Wyoming with his award-winning wife and co-author, Kathleen O'Neal Gear, and a charming sheltie named, Jake.

# about kathleen o'neal gear

**Kathleen O'Neal Gear** is a *New York Times* bestselling author of fifty-seven books and a national award-winning archaeologist. The U.S. Department of the Interior has awarded her two Special Achievement awards for outstanding management of America's cultural resources.

In 2015 the United States Congress honored her with a Certificate of Special Congressional Recognition, and the California State Legislature passed Joint Member Resolution #117 saying, "The contributions of Kathleen O'Neal Gear to the fields of history, archaeology, and writing have been invaluable…"

In 2021 she received the Owen Wister Award for lifetime contributions to western literature, and in 2023 received the Frank Waters Award for "a body of work representing excellence in writing and storytelling that embodies the spirit of the American West."